"FREE! FREE! FREE!" THE VOICE OF TYPHON BOOMED.

Glynis felt power rush out of the conch into the ocean. Offshore, a mass of water started to swell, rising up and taking on shape as it grew taller. Forty, fifty, a hundred feet it rose up from the waves, taking on a human shape to loom over the shore. Glynis tried to scream, but terror choked her. *It's from my dreams!*

The man-shaped mountain of water that was Typhon lifted his mighty arms, one at a time, and the waves lifted in response. He clenched a fist, and a bolt of lightning arced down from the sky to blast a rock on the beach. "THE POWERS OF THE STORM PRIMEVAL ARE MINE AGAIN! THE CLEANSING OF THE WORLD SHALL BEGIN!"

ARE YOU AFRAID OF THE DARK?™ novels

Available from MINSTREL Books

THE TALE OF
THE SHIMMERING SHELL

DAVID CODY WEISS AND BOBBI JG WEISS

A MINSTREL® BOOK

PUBLISHED BY POCKET BOOKS

New York   London   Toronto   Sydney   Tokyo   Singapore

This book is a work of fiction. Names, characters, places and incidents are products of the author's imagination or are used fictitiously. Any resemblance to actual events or locales or persons, living or dead, is entirely coincidental.

A MINSTREL PAPERBACK *Original*

 A Minstrel Book published by
POCKET BOOKS, a division of Simon & Schuster Inc.
1230 Avenue of the Americas, New York, NY 10020

ISBN: 0-671-00392-5

First Minstrel Books printing March 1997

10 9 8 7 6 5 4 3 2 1

Cover art by John Youssi

Printed in the U.S.A.

For Nat and Edie . . .
things turned out for the best after all.

PROLOGUE: THE MIDNIGHT SOCIETY

Wish you weren't afraid of the dark? Come a little closer. The fire will keep it at bay—for a while. You may wish it were a brighter fire. You may wish it would last a little longer. But it's all that we've got and we'll have to make do with it.

We? We're the Midnight Society and I'm Sam. I'm here to tell you that there are wishes and then there are wishes. Don't understand? Well . . .

Did you ever hear the old saying, "Be careful what you wish for—it might come true?" Well, if Glynis Barrons had paid attention to that advice, she might not have had such a scary time at the beach. But then we wouldn't have had a scary story to tell you.

Glynis was literally Not a Happy Camper.

Think of a summer vacation on an island beach.

1

Swimming. Hiking. Finding seashells. Meeting new people. This all might sound great to you, but because Glynis had to share it with her new stepbrother, she thought that anything *in the world would be better.*

She was wrong. Things could be a lot *worse.*

So pull up a stone. Take your shoes off and stick your bare feet in the warm sand near the fire. Imagine you're at the beach. But be careful what you pick up.

Submitted for the approval of the Midnight Society, I call this story . . . THE TALE OF THE SHIMMERING SHELL.

CHAPTER
1

Glynis Barrons clomped down the beach, her new waffle-stompers scattering sand and driftwood at every stride. To her right, Strike's Peak gnawed into the setting sun, giving the sky a strange yellowish overtone. To her left, clouds churned far out over the gray Atlantic and threatened to turn a sultry August day into a chilly island night.

She scowled at the watch on her wrist, bound there by a homemade band of plaited straw. It would serve Todd right if she couldn't find him and he missed dinner. Maybe being cold and hungry would get it through his thick skull that he was supposed to keep track of time himself instead of making Glynis have to fetch him home before dark.

Glynis snorted. Of all the possible stepbrothers in the world, why did she have to get Todd? The dweeb was somewhere down the beach, probably watching the wriggling of slimy slugs or bugs or some other pointless "Wonder of Nature" that he was always babbling about. She could kind of understand why he went overboard on that stuff—after all, Todd had been raised in a big city. Concrete was practically the only thing he saw before Todd's mother had married Glynis's dad. But having to give up her own time to track Todd down wasn't fair.

That's really the heart of the problem, thought Glynis. *I'm the one who always has to give things up because of the "new arrangement."*

Before her father's remarriage, Glynis and Michael Barrons had been tight, a "me and you against the world" team. Glynis had kept house and fixed dinner for her dad when he came home from work, setting the table neatly with fresh-cut flowers from the garden. Together they had gone on long Sunday drives, and Michael had made time to be at every one of Glynis's softball games during the season. Summer vacations had always been an opportunity for the two of them to explore some new patch of woods or to swim and snorkel at some beach.

But this year, and *this* beach . . . Glynis looked around her as she walked. She realized that her dad had intended this vacation to be an opportunity to let the new family get to know each other better. But what had possessed him to book them all into a lonely cottage on Seawrack Island? Glynis thought that the barrier island's only qualification for beach resort status was that it actually *had* a beach. And a cold, pebbly beach at that.

The gray-green Atlantic surged rhythmically, heaving itself against stones worn smooth by the eternal dance. Uphill along the beach, bleached sea grass, bobbing cattails, and scrubby brush marked the disputed territory between land life and sea life. Wavy lines of high and low tide marks sketched a history of skirmishes, advances and retreats in the struggle between the pounding ocean and resisting land.

A line of low hills marked the spine of the island, carpeted with grass and low trees bent backward by constant winds. Glynis let her eyes follow the hills as they rose toward Strike's Peak, the highest point on the island.

Just as the ocean dominated the eastern view, so Strike's Peak dominated the western, a craggy mass of rock that had been upthrust ages ago. At the top of the peak stood an ancient, gnarled oak tree. Its trunk had been blasted by the frequent lightning bolts that gave the hill its name. Glynis shaded her eyes with her hand and studied the old oak carefully. Something about it seemed odd, tickling the back of her mind.

Despite its lightning-scarred appearance, the scorched tree was not dead. Leaves grew in tufts at the ends of twisted branches. Angry bolts from the sky had split the trunk in several places but the tree still clung stubbornly to life.

There! That's it! Glynis stopped short. Something had gleamed briefly at the base of the tree. There was a quick glimmer of red-purple, as if the dying sunlight had reflected off a shiny object. What could it be?

The wind shifted, misting Glynis with ocean spray, the sudden chill making her shiver. *Oh, great,* she thought, looking at dark clouds building at the far edge of the ocean, *the perfect addition to a perfect vacation—a storm!* Glynis didn't mind rain during the summer—on a hot day it could be great. But the idea of a storm building up over a thousand miles of ocean and rushing headlong toward her—*NOT my idea of fun!*

She sneered. *Yet another wonderful attraction of scenic Seawrack Island! I'd better find Todd, pronto.*

Glynis hurried toward a low hill just ahead. Perhaps from its crest she'd be able to see Todd farther down the island.

The steep slope stretched her calf muscles and made her thighs ache, but the strain felt good. Glynis liked exertion; it made her feel like she was accomplishing something. She liked things neat and orderly and preferred tackling problems head on. She had always thought her life would run in a predictable manner and had no patience for sudden changes and complications.

When she got to the hilltop, the southeastern curve of Seawrack Island stretched out before her eyes. Like a hook, its southern tip turned back upon itself, forming a small cove. Glynis could see all the way to the island's end. Squinting her eyes, Glynis scanned the shore for the safety orange of Todd's vest.

There might have been a spot of bright color far ahead, but it didn't move. *Right,* she thought. *Why should anything be easy today?* Stepping crabwise down the sandy side of the hill, Glynis started southward.

Rounding a hill, she came upon the only other dwelling on this end of Seawrack. It was an ancient-looking bungalow built right into the hillside, its wide front deck hanging out over the sloping beachfront and held up by tall posts. It made Glynis feel uneasy.

That creepy old lady is there again. Glynis wasn't usually quick to judge strangers, but in the three days that she had been on the island this woman had struck her as being very odd. She couldn't put her finger on why, though. The old woman looked innocent enough. *But she just sits there all day staring at the ocean, never moving,* Glynis thought. *She's like one of those old seaman's wives, watching and waiting for someone who's never coming back.*

Glynis shook off the fantasy. Still, she hurried past the little house, hoping the old woman wouldn't notice her. She needn't have worried— the woman didn't move, didn't blink. She just sat there, wrapped in a faded plaid shawl, staring out to sea. Somehow Glynis knew that those staring eyes were a deep sea-blue-green.

The creepy feeling returned. *I can barely see her face from this distance,* she thought, *let alone her eye color.* Then she saw a gleam of brilliant greenish blue at the old woman's throat, a flash so bright yet so quick she wasn't sure she'd seen anything. *Okay, that's it,* she snorted. *The minute I'm back home I'm getting my eyes examined!*

Glynis finally reached the top of the far hill. She scanned the beach ahead, muttering, "C'mon,

8

you little cretin, where are you?" Then she spotted him. From her vantage point on the hill she could see all of the small cove that formed the hook of the island.

There, facedown on the sand with his head in a pool of water, was Todd.

CHAPTER 2

Glynis raced down the hill like the wind, but it seemed to take an eternity. The sand caught at her feet like flypaper. Clumps of sea grass and half buried horseshoe crab shells poked up from the ground to trip her. Even the air felt thicker, as if trying to slow her down. Her heart felt like it was going to burst before she reached Todd. *If that little dweeb gets hurt out here, Dad'll never forgive me!*

Ten yards from Todd's body, Glynis's foot snagged on a piece of driftwood. As she toppled forward, she threw her hands up to protect her face. Remembering her training from gym classes, she tucked herself into a ball so she would roll

10

out of the fall instead of landing flat. Even so, she hit hard on her left arm and had the breath knocked out of her as she went tumbling down the beach. The world faded to black and back to light again.

As she lay on her back gasping for breath, a shadow fell over her. A dark form with glassy staring eyes loomed over her, wet tendrils swinging in the air, water dripping. Its mouth sputtered, spraying Glynis's face. "You okay, Glynnie?" Todd asked.

Glynis's heart stopped in her chest. *Am I dead too? Did the fall break my neck? Are Todd and I ghosts now?* On second thought, Glynis realized that ghosts probably didn't wear scuba goggles and have mucus dripping from their noses. Grossing out, thinking stopped and fury set in.

Glynis staggered to her feet. "You creep! What kind of stupid stunt was that?" Her left shoulder hurt and her wrist felt like raw hamburger. "I thought you had drowned!"

Todd stepped back in surprise. "What do you mean? I was just checking out the tide pools." He pulled his black rubber goggles off, nearly snagging the strap in his curly brown hair. "I forgot to bring my snorkel with me, so I had to hold my breath to see." His face lit up. "But I found a batch of cowries!"

Glynis gawked at him. Was Todd so clueless that he couldn't see that he'd scared the pants off her? All she could do was repeat, "Cowries . . . ?"

"You know," Todd said as he dug into the pocket of his shorts. "Cowry shells." He held out a handful of inch-long ovals, like shiny plastic beads with toothy mouths smiling up at her. "The Indians used them for decoration and trading," he beamed. "Like money. I found these Atlantic Yellows on the beach and there are live Measled Cowries over in that pool." Todd looked dreamily at the ocean. "Isn't it cool to think that you can find stuff like this, just like people did hundreds, even thousands of years ago?" He sighed. "It's like time standing still."

Glynis resisted the urge to slap the shells out of Todd's hand. "Time can stand still for you, space-case, but the rest of us live in the real world!" She dug Todd's watch out of her jacket pocket and threw it at him. "And in the real world we remember our own watches so we can come home to dinner on time without having to be *fetched!*"

Todd's face fell as he caught the watch in mid-air. "Sorry about that, Sis." He stared at the brightly colored band instead of at her. "I realized I'd forgotten that, too, after I was out here, but

12

I figured I could keep track of the time by watching the sun."

Todd's apology only worsened Glynis's mood. "My name is not 'Sis,' " she barked. "It's Glynis! I'm a person, not a job description. Your mother may have married my father, but that's not gonna change who and what I am." Glynis clenched her jaw shut so fast she almost bit her tongue.

Even though Todd was nearly as tall as she was, he seemed to shrink in reaction to her words. *I shouldn't have said that,* she thought ruefully. But then her irritation returned. *Why does he have to drive me so crazy all the time?*

Todd turned away from her and stared out at the restless ocean, dark clouds rimming the horizon. "Yeah, you're probably right," he mumbled. "It's late and we should be getting back." He stuffed the shells back in his pocket and then dusted sand off his hands.

Glynis felt a knot in her stomach turn flip-flops. Anger and embarrassment wrestled inside as she fought to control her feelings. However she felt about her new family situation, she knew she had stepped over the line by saying things out loud. *That's the game you're supposed to play. Pretend everything's okay and keep your feelings all bottled up.* She clenched and opened her fists, taking deep breaths—clench, relax, breathe . . . clench, relax, breathe . . .

Todd gave a stage cough, trying to get her attention. She looked up at him. He fidgeted and then pointed at her left hand. "Uh, maybe you should do something about that," he said awkwardly.

Glynis looked down and gasped. There was a raw patch from her wrist halfway up her forearm where rough stones had scraped her when she'd fallen. Beads of blood welled up from the deeper places in the wound. But that was not what took Glynis's breath away. The sharp rocks had also torn through the carefully plaited straw of her watchband. "Oh, no!" she moaned. "It took me hours to make that!"

She glared at Todd, furious. "That's it! You get your butt back to the bungalow!" She jabbed the watchband at him. "I don't want to even *see* you until I've gotten this fixed—and maybe not even then!"

Todd's mouth hung open at his stepsister's fierceness. When he continued to stand there, not moving, Glynis really exploded. "You're just hopeless!" she shrieked. She turned away and stalked back up the hill.

After a few steps she sneaked a look back. Todd was still standing on the beach, staring down at his feet. He had made no move in any direction. *Does he think I'm going to come back? Doesn't he realize what he did?* Glynis set her jaw. *I have better things to do than play sheepdog for him!*

But it wasn't until she was halfway to Strike's Peak that her temper cooled and she realized that she *didn't* have anything better to do. But it was too late to turn back now. Besides, Todd was still down on the beach, slowly scuffling his way back home. *I might as well keep on going to the top,* Glynis thought. *I've never been there and maybe a stiff climb will make me feel like I've accomplished* something *today!*

When she reached the peak Glynis was surprised to find herself short of breath but still seething with anger. Normally the stretch and pull of her muscles left Glynis feeling refreshed. Exercise cleared her mind and chased away bad moods. Not today, however.

Wind and storm had exposed the upper roots of the lightning-blasted oak crowning the hill. Glynis sat down on one of the gnarled humps and leaned back against the tree. The scrape on her arm had stopped bleeding but it still throbbed painfully. Taking care not to hurt herself more, she unbuckled her watch to inspect the damage to the strap.

The strap was made of straw, plaited in a Peruvian-style six-strand braid. When Glynis had told Todd that it had taken hours to make she'd been telling the truth. It wasn't that the plaiting was difficult. Rather, Glynis had done and redone each step of the braiding process until she felt that her fingers knew the moves without looking. Something about taking loose straw—a common and almost ugly material—and making a beautiful, tightly woven strap gave her a surprising sense of satisfaction.

And now it was ruined.

Well, not really ruined. Glynis could unravel the strap and replace the torn strands in just a little time. She just resented having her creation spoiled in the first place.

"I wish I could just make them all go away and leave me alone!" she suddenly yelled aloud. The intensity in her voice surprised her and rocked her back.

"Ouch!" A rough point poked her between the shoulder blades. She jerked forward again.

Angry at the brief pain—angry at everything—Glynis reached down and tugged at a handful of long grass. Unconsciously, her fingers started to

16

automatically sort the tall stalks into even bunches.

It's just not fair, she moaned to herself, folding the outside left bunch inward over a second bunch and under a third. *I had everything under control until Dad married Jaye.* And she had, too. Although she was only fourteen, Glynis had managed to juggle schoolwork and housekeeping every day so that she could have dinner waiting for her father when he came home from work. She tried to keep her dad's non-business time as tidy and worry-free as possible. The payoff for all that effort came on weekends and vacation, when Michael and Glynis would go out together walking in the woods or driving up and down the coast looking for empty beaches and out-of-the-way curiosities.

It was just a year before at Old Williamsburg in Virginia that Glynis first discovered plaiting and finger weaving. She had expected the place to be a sort of Early American Disneyland, but it turned out to be more. Dedicated to showing how early American settlers had lived and worked, it was an authentic restored village populated by people who dressed in seventeenth century clothes and practiced a variety of industries and crafts as their ancestors had done three centuries before.

17

Glynis was fascinated by how self-sufficient the village was. From just the materials found in nearby woods or grown by their own farmers these people made everything they needed to survive from scratch. She could have sat watching the women who spun thread and wove cloth for hours. But it was when an eight-year-old braided straw together to make an "instant" egg basket that something inside Glynis had cried, *Yes!*

As soon as she got back home Glynis raided the library for books about plaiting. The more she learned, the more she felt that she had found something important to her. Learning how to make things herself from materials at hand made her feel as self-sufficient as she imagined strong women of the past to be. This feeling was reinforced when she discovered that braiding and plaiting were among the oldest of the civilized arts. In fact, she learned that braiding, plaiting, and weaving were all the same technique—the terms were different to indicate the materials used. Weaving meant that thread was being used, while braiding meant hair or strips of cloth or leather, and plaiting indicated that straw or flax was used.

Ancient cultures had valued these humble crafts so highly that they included them in their myths and legends. They marked objects as sacred or

18

special by weaving special covers for them. The ancient Greeks believed that the Fates spun the thread of existence and wove it into the cloth of life. Cutting that thread meant ending that life. The ancient Egyptians had carried this even further—they buried their dead in fine linen, weaving strips of it around the body to create a mummy. They felt that by wrapping the body securely it would be sealed and preserved for eternity.

One of Glynis's early projects had been a pair of placemats she had braided out of scraps of old linen sheets. It made her feel good to set them on the table each night, knowing she had made something useful out of material that would have just been thrown away. *Sort of like giving it a second chance at life,* she beamed.

And braiding gave Glynis something to retreat to during those unsettled months after her dad had met and married Jaye. She knew that she had no right to upset her father's new happiness, but she couldn't understand why her life had to be disrupted by it.

At the thought of Jaye and Todd, Glynis sighed heavily and leaned back. She lurched forward just as quickly—she had forgotten about that sharp point in the trunk of the tree. The sudden pain broke her out of her daydreaming.

She looked down and saw that she had been braiding grass unconsciously while sitting in front of the tree. *Well,* she thought wryly, *if I'm lost on a desert island or in some kind of disaster, I know I won't be completely helpless . . .*

Then she noticed that she had a clear view down to the strange old woman's house at the foot of the hill. *She's still sitting right where she was.* Glynis frowned. *What is with her?* In spite of the fact that it must have been getting cold on the sun deck now that the hill was casting its shadow over the bungalow, the old woman still kept her vigil. Was she waiting for a signal that only she would recognize in the clouds gathering over the Atlantic?

As if on cue, the old woman suddenly moved. But she didn't rise up out of her chair. Instead, she and the chair moved as a unit back toward the house, disappearing from sight behind the roof peak. *She's in a wheelchair,* Glynis realized with amazement. *Maybe she sits there all day watching because she can't do anything else. So much for the great mystery.* Glynis slumped back on the tree.

She had forgotten about the sharp point again. "Ouch!" she yelped, snapping forward. "What keeps poking me?"

Glynis turned around to look at the tree trunk.

There was an irregular lump in the bark with something protruding where the bark had weathered away. A mass of dark fibers stuck upward from the tree with something light colored breaking through its tip. It didn't look like wood at all. She felt it. Underneath the fibers was something hard and smooth, like polished stone or glass. Glynis picked away at the covering, which crumbled to dusty scraps as she tugged at it. She thought she saw a crisscross pattern to the scraps, but the wind blew them away before she could examine them closely.

It's a seashell, she marveled. *There's a seashell stuck in a solid tree!* Even in the fading light of the day she could see that its surface shimmered with an iridescent pattern, like the mother-of-pearl inside oysters. Without thinking, she pressed her finger to the point. It was sharp enough to draw blood. "Yeow!" she snatched her hand back and sucked on her wounded finger. *Swift move, Glynis,* she thought. *You're really bent on self-destructing today.* A bitter taste hit her tongue and her vision rippled for a moment. A flash of multicolored light seemed to burst from the shell, increasing Glynis's dizziness.

She shook her head to clear it. *I must really be letting all this Todd stuff stress me out,* she thought, *to let a flash of sunlight on a shell make me get all light-headed.* Sunlight? What time *was* it?

Her watch lay forgotten in her left hand. *Oh no! It's almost dinnertime!* She scrambled down the hill. *I came out here to fetch Todd for dinner. I'll look like a complete dork if I'm the one who's late now!*

It wasn't until she was almost home that she remembered that the setting sun had already been behind Strike's Peak, leaving her in shadow when the half-buried shell had flashed in her eyes.

Where had the light come from?

CHAPTER 3

The long shadows of the hills stretched down the beach and were nipping at the surf by the time Glynis arrived at her family's rented bungalow. Warm light glowed from the windows as she ran up the porch steps. Breathlessly she yanked the screen door open and barreled inside.

"You're home," Michael Barrons greeted her. He was a tall, dignified-looking man with salt-and-pepper hair. At the moment, he looked comical wearing oversized mitts to hold a steaming casserole dish. "We'd about given you up for lost." Glynis's stepmother, Jaye, used a cloth napkin to take the casserole from her husband and put it on a mat on the table. A lump swelled in Glynis's throat as she recognized the mat—it was one of the two she had woven for placemats. Its mate sat nearby under a centerpiece of dried flowers. Jaye caught the direction of Glynis's stare.

"Your father showed me your work," Jaye said. "They're too beautiful not to use." Jaye repositioned the flower bowl so that it was perfectly centered on the mat. "Of course, since there are only two mats, I had to use them for the centerpiece and the serving bowl. Maybe you can make two more, so we can use them as placemats for all of us."

Glynis couldn't think of an answer. Memories of mealtimes back home flooded her mind. Memories of Glynis and her father laughing together over dinners she had cooked and served on those placemats on a table set for two. Just two. Now the table was set for four and the placemats were plain paper.

Jaye and Michael finished laying out dinner in an unconscious dance, her busy motions counterbalanced by his slower, more deliberate moves. Then they pulled their chairs out and sat down. Michael glanced at Glynis. "Need an invitation?" he murmured.

"I . . . I'll be ready in a second," Glynis choked out. She stumbled toward the hallway.

Without warning, Todd zipped around the corner and nearly collided with her. "Whoops!" he yipped. "I didn't know this was a slowpoke-crossing zone!" He spun neatly around Glynis, lifting a large cardboard box above his head to avoid hitting her. Glynis's eyes widened at the sight of that box.

Michael looked up from serving the casserole. "I thought we were going to wait until after dinner to see your trophies, Todd."

"I just wanted to show you how I've arranged them, Dad," replied Todd, setting the box down.

Glynis exploded. "Daddeee!" she squeaked in outrage. "That's my boot box! What is he doing with *my* boot box?"

Todd flinched.

Michael raised an eyebrow. "Todd needed something to store his shell collection in for the time being," he said. "This was empty."

"But it's for my boots! It's the box they came in and no other box fits them just right." Glynis knew she was being whiny, but she couldn't help it.

"Don't be silly, sweetheart," Jaye smiled. "You live in those boots." She poured milk into a glass and set it before the empty chair. "Now come and have your dinner."

Glynis plopped down into the designated chair. "What's the big deal about shells anyway?" she grumped. "If they're so wonderful, why do the animals throw them away?"

Todd set the boot box under his chair before sitting down to eat. "They don't. Not while they're alive, anyway."

"The shells are actually attached to them, aren't they?" Jaye asked.

"Yup," Todd said around a forkful. "It's calcium carbonate—lime. The animals—they're called mollusks—secrete it as they grow. That's what makes the stripe and ring patterns." He grinned, pleased with his own knowledge.

Glynis groaned to herself, suspecting the ten-year-old was launching into a lecture. She was right.

"Mollusks are like snails," Todd continued enthusiastically. "They're ninety percent sea water. So are human beings, for that matter. Anyway, they make shells to protect them from enemies and stuff. It really works, too, because there are more kinds of mollusks in the world than any other kind of animals except insects. There's over a hundred and fifty *thousand* kinds of mollusks that have been identified." Todd beamed. "They've been around for millions and millions of years."

To Glynis's surprise, her father encouraged Todd's lecture. "In fact, it was the finding of fossilized seashells on the tops of mountains that made geologists realize that the Earth wasn't always the same—it changed over time. Ancient shells made limestone on seabeds. Then those beds rose up to become mountains and whole continents sank to become new oceans."

Jaye was taking a second helping as she asked, "Is that where the lime I use in the garden comes from?"

"Yup," said Todd. "Same stuff. You get it from cooking limestone in an oven. And limestone is just billions of ancient shells crunched and pressed for millions of years until they became rock." He wolfed another forkful. "You can burn fresh shells for lime, too," he added.

Since the dinner conversation was obviously going to revolve around Todd tonight, Glynis lowered her head and plowed through her food. *Isn't school supposed to be out for summer?* The conversation ran on without her, but nobody seemed to notice.

She found herself wondering how the adults could listen to Todd rattle on without noticing that he kept talking with food in his mouth. *It's amazing how he gets away with it! They must expect little boys to be messy and don't even bother to try and stop it.*

Jaye was looking down into Todd's box. "These

27

are beautiful! It's a wonder that such pretty things can be so useful."

"And, it's used for more than just gardens, Mom," said Todd. "Without lime, there'd be no cement for building. But people have used whole shells throughout history, too. They used them for ornaments and prizes and symbols of office . . ."

"And trumpets, if I remember correctly," finished Michael. "There was a mural of an undersea palace in the art museum back home. The king was painted as blowing a conch shell like a horn."

Jaye turned to Glynis and teased, "Maybe you could help Todd find a conch shell for us to blow so you two won't be late for dinner again."

I wouldn't have been late if it weren't for him, Glynis was about to say, but her stepbrother cut in too fast.

"Not a chance! Conches live in warm tropical water. You wouldn't see one this far north. They like deep water, too. The waters here are really shallow for miles and miles out. It's called the continental . . . um . . ." His voice faded as he groped for the term.

Glynis smiled to herself. *So, Nature Boy doesn't have all the answers after all.* But then her father came to the dork's rescue.

"Shelf, son. It's the continental shelf." He

smiled at the boy. "But I'm pleased. You've done quite a bit of research."

"That's only the beginning . . . Dad." Todd positively glowed under the praise. He hadn't quite gotten used to Michael's new status as his stepfather. "Now that I'm starting a collection of my own, I'm going to divide them into categories and make labels and learn lots more."

Jaye patted her son's hand. "You could go to college and become a marine biologist someday."

Glynis's food was gone and so was her patience. "Will I have to wait that long to get my boot box back?" she snapped. There was silence around the table. Then Michael Barrons spoke.

"Glynis, what is the matter with you? Todd is just borrowing your box. Does it hurt you to share a little?"

It was all too much for Glynis. Tears welled up in her eyes. "How much do I have to share, Daddy? He's borrowing my box and he's borrowing my father. Is he going to borrow my whole *life* next?" She leaped out of her chair and headed for the bedroom. She paused before the door and turned back, sobbing. "Why can't you all just go away and leave me alone!"

She fled into the bedroom, slamming the door behind her.

CHAPTER 4

Glynis couldn't even sulk in privacy. With only two bedrooms in the bungalow, there was no escaping Todd. If he wasn't actually there asleep in the other twin bed, traces of him were scattered all over the room. Glynis looked at the clutter on the floor in annoyance. *I'm never going to survive a whole week of this!*

She threw herself onto her bed and buried her head under a pile of pillows. Safe under the covers, she burst into tears. *I wish they would all stop making my life miserable!*

She sobbed herself to sleep long before Todd shuffled into bed.

*　　*　　*

It was the sound of the surf that caught her attention first.

Once Glynis roused herself enough to identify the sound, she realized that she was standing knee-deep in surging water. Or rather, from the knees down she *was* the water. What felt odd about it was that she *didn't* feel odd about it. It seemed perfectly natural to her. *Todd was saying something about people being mostly sea water earlier,* she thought. *So the little dweeb was right about something after all.*

Thinking of the main irritant in her life, she looked around, expecting to see him grinning in triumph at her admission. All she saw was the beach of Seawrack Island, empty of any sign of human life. *Where'd the bungalow go?* she wondered. The rented home was nowhere in sight. *Looks like I'm alone at last.*

Strangely enough, she didn't feel bothered by the absence of her family. Her awareness spread out to fill the emptiness. She enjoyed being the only person on the beach, possibly the only person on the island. For a while she just basked in the feeling.

And then Glynis noticed marks in the sand a few yards to the south. It looked like a crowd of people had milled about at the edge of the water. From that scuffling, a lone set of footprints led inland. Her sense of comfortable solitude vanished. *I knew this was too good to be true.*

She left the surf and followed the footsteps, her normal legs and feet appearing as she moved out of the water.

Without apparent transition she was suddenly walking up a valley toward Strike's Peak. Something about the place nagged at Glynis's memory. *I've been here before, but something's missing.* Then she knew the answer: *This is where that old lady's house is supposed to be!*

But there was no sign of the house. In fact, it was apparent that no human dwelling had ever stood among the scrub and grass. Instead, a small cave yawned at the upper notch of the little valley. The line of footprints led straight to the cave. Glynis felt compelled to follow.

The cave was a narrow, winding thing, burrowing deep into the spine of the island. Oddly, Glynis found herself able to see the rough walls clearly, even though there was no light to see by. The cave cut through rocks that looked like tall stripes sloppily painted up the wall. As she walked, she noticed a strange sound rising around her. Rising up from the rocks themselves, it whispered like a choir chanting something just below the range of hearing.

There are people here, Glynis thought, and

turned to look back the way she had come. But instead of a clear, narrow path back into daylight, all that was behind her was a wall of solid rock. Her chest clutched with panic. *I'm trapped!*

Blackness washed over her, blotting out time and space. Her panic rose, pushing against the thick nothingness. *Let me out of here!* she screamed inside her head. Her cry echoed in the void, multiplying upon itself until it was a chorus shouting "Let me out of here!"

Then something answered.

It was more a mental awareness of Something Else than anything Glynis saw or heard. "Help me!" she shouted.

"HELP ME!" echoed back to her. But it was an echo that rumbled like a truckload of gravel being dumped.

Suddenly the blackness thickened into a dense, clinging blankct. It started moving, carrying Glynis along with it. She felt herself tugged along by a current, squeezing upward through cracks, every particle of her being yearning for freedom. The more she struggled upward, the faster the current moved. She felt the Other's desire match her own and lend its strength to hers.

With a sudden snapping feeling, she found herself standing on the windswept crest of Strike's Peak. A windstorm spun mist and debris in a spiral around the great, lightning-blasted oak. Glynis felt so relieved to be out in the open again that she threw herself against the tree and hugged the rough bark.

She heard the sound of the sea again and felt her body take on the same watery quality it had started with, back when she'd stood in the surf. *It's like I'm not just made of sea water,* she thought, *but that the ocean itself is inside me!* As she gripped the tree, her hands began to weep sea water. The water ran in streams down the bark onto the strange lump that had poked her earlier in the day.

Glynis stared—the lump was drinking in the water like a sponge! And like a sponge, it began to swell within the tree. A rippling rainbow of light burst out of the lump and blinded her with its brilliance.

When her eyes cleared, she gasped in wonder.

The hilltop and the tree still stood before her as it had a moment before, but now they had been magically transported to the bottom of the sea. Ripples of green light swept over the sea bottom beyond the hill, and schools of fish shivered by in a stream of liquid metal. Glynis's hair floated in the currents and she realized that she was still breathing in spite of being underwater.

Oh, I get it—this is a dream! She smiled to herself. *A* weird *dream, but kind of fun!*

A great rumbling chuckle shook the seabed like an earthquake. *OF COURSE IT'S A DREAM, LITTLE ONE,* a voice grated. *BUT ARE YOU DREAMING OF ME OR AM I DREAMING OF YOU?*

The hill jerked out from under Glynis, toppling her backward in slow motion down to the level seabed. Wrenching itself upward, the hill began changing shape as it grew taller. It seemed to gather substance from the ocean around it, sand filling out a body, seaweed clinging like hair and clothing, and a single shining conch shell winking at her like an eye in its massive face. When it seemed to Glynis that things couldn't get any stranger, a small figure came torpedoing through the water from above. *Todd?* Glynis thought in shock. *What's* he *doing in my dream?*

Todd stopped to float between Glynis and the mountain-thing, his right hand holding out something that blazed bright green, like new growth in springtime. The mountain-thing recoiled and Todd waved the green thing at it again. The mountain-thing started to slump back into the mud.

Glynis balled her fists. *He's spoiling my dream! Can't he leave* anything *of mine alone?* A shout burst from her lungs. "Go away, Todd! Go away! Go away!"

Her shout sped through the water like great ripples of power. The ripples struck the enormous sea-thing and brought a great toothy smile to its face. *GRANTED,* it bellowed and swept a massive, seaweedy arm out toward Todd.

Before Glynis could react, the hand grabbed Todd's body, knocking the blazing green out of his grasp to tumble to the depths. Continuing in a majestic sweep, the hand brought Todd up to the gaping mouth and popped him inside like a tasty snack.

No! That's not what I meant! she shrieked, as a horrible crunching sound filled her ears.

Glynis bolted upright in bed, gasping uncontrollably. Still panicked, her eyes shot to the other bed. Todd lay sleeping peacefully, gentle snores murmuring as he breathed.

Glynis swallowed, trying to calm down. *What a nightmare!* The tug of clammy clothes reminded her that she'd fallen asleep still dressed. *Yeesh! I'm drenched in sweat,* she thought. *No wonder I feel soggy.* Silently she changed her clothes and snuggled under the covers.

But sleep was a long time coming.

CHAPTER 5

The sun had drifted halfway up the sky by the time Glynis woke. She lay in bed, eyes closed, and let her sleepy mind drift. Though usually energetic, she still enjoyed that short half-dreaming, half-awake period each morning. "Lounge minutes" she liked to call them. *Just about the only time I really get to myself nowadays,* she thought. In their effort to cement the new family together, Michael and Jaye kept thinking up a constant stream of "family activities" for them all to participate in.

Tattered shreds of the strange dream she'd had the night before floated up to her conscious mind. *Isn't that just like dreams?* she wondered as she groped to piece the fragments together. *They're so clear when you have them but they fall apart when you try to remember them.* All she could recall was a faint image of Todd being swallowed up by some kind of monster. Somehow, the bright sunlight made the image seem comical instead of horrific. *The next time he's out of line, I should tell him that a sea monster's gonna get him!*

She opened her eyes and looked across the room to gloat at Todd's sleeping form. His bed was empty, however. *That's weird—he's already up. Normally he has to be pried out of bed!* Odder still was the fact that the bed was made up neatly and the clutter was gone from the floor.

Glynis cocked an ear but heard no sounds of movement or conversation in the bungalow. Only then did she notice the steep angle of the sunlight pouring in through the bedroom window. *Wow! I must have* really *overslept!* She snatched her robe from the foot of the bed and padded out to the kitchen.

"Dad? Jaye? Todd?" No one answered her calls. For a moment the empty house felt somehow connected to her half-remembered dream. A chill swept over her as if a cloud had covered the sun. Her heart skipped a beat.

Then her eye fell upon a note propped up on

the kitchen table. In Jaye's neat script Glynis read:

> *Glyn,*
> *Dad and I are going out boating this morning. Don't expect to be back until late afternoon. Keep an eye on Todd and try to relax and have fun, dear.*
>
> *Mom*

The signature bothered Glynis. Jaye was trying awfully hard to make the new family arrangement work smoothly, but little things like this still jarred. "You're not my mother," she said aloud to the empty room.

Glynis knew the blunt statement was unkind, but she continued brooding about it while she made herself breakfast. Somewhere deep inside her all the dissatisfactions that had been building came together into a smoldering lump. "This whole vacation thing was a big mistake," she declared, buttering a slice of raisin toast.

Sure, the idea had been to spend a week at a remote spot so that everyone could get adjusted to the new family situation without distractions. *But I don't want to adjust to anything! Can't they see that? If I can't have my life back the way it was, I just want to be left alone!*

At least this morning she would get her wish.

She ate alone on the porch, her only company a dirty gray seagull who patrolled the rail, squawking for a handout. "Sorry, mac," she said, licking her fingers clean. "Better luck somewhere else."

The idea of "somewhere else" struck Glynis as a good one, so she walked north to what passed for "town" on Seawrack Island—a small collection of weathered buildings that were home to bait shops, antique stores, and little craftsy boutiques that sold touristy stuff to visitors. At the far end of the boardwalk lay a round arcade garishly labeled "The Beach House." Filled with pinball and video games, it was the hangout of choice on the island.

But the tourist kids looked geeky, and the small crowd of locals hung out in one corner and sneered at everyone else. Glynis had never felt so shut out in her life. The smoldering knot inside her grew hotter. *How could my own dad do this to me?* she fumed.

She vented her unhappiness by hiking around the south end of the island. The inland shore was steep and rocky, and at the south point, seaswept and slippery. The tough, challenging hike took Glynis quite a while and left her tired enough to stop for a rest well short of making it back home. Tired, but still restless.

Panting, she sat on a rock and hung her head between her knees. As she rested, Glynis stared down at the pebbly beach beneath her feet. Large rounded gray and slate-colored stones lay clumped between patches of fine sand and light-colored bits. With a start, Glynis recognized that the bits were tiny seashell fragments.

Seashells reminded her of Todd, of course, and she lifted her head to look up the beach. *Todd's tide pools are just over that rise. I wonder if he's got his head in them again today?* She glanced over at the ocean. *It's low tide! He'd have his head stuck in mud if he was there now!* She laughed out loud at the mental picture of Eager Beaver Boy with his head in a mud puddle.

Nah, not even Todd's *that dumb,* she concluded. But out of curiosity, she now *had* to check it out.

Todd wasn't at the tide pools, muddy or not. Glynis stood on the beach, unsure of what to do next. With no one to talk to and nothing to occupy her time, she almost envied Todd's preoccupation with shells. There was nothing here for *her.* Absolutely nothing.

Then she remembered the strange lump imbedded in the oak on Strike's Peak. And now that she remembered it, she wondered how she could ever have forgotten about it. Its presence on the hilltop far above now pulled at her curiosity, like the tugging of a string. She turned toward the tug and started climbing the hill.

Glynis had gone only a hundred yards or so when a shout stopped her.

"Hey, Glynis!"

Oh, that voice. All too familiar, all too annoying. Glynis gritted her teeth and turned. Sure enough, there was Todd, waving up at her like a human semaphore. Glynis was so irritated at the sight of him that it took a few seconds for it to sink in where the boy was waving *from*—the sundeck of the old woman's house! He was sitting next to her at a rickety-looking card table.

Leave it to Todd to make friends with the local weird woman, Glynis thought, and frowned. *Good for him. Maybe it'll keep him out of my hair!*

Glynis was about to continue her climb, when the old woman looked up and smiled at her. For a second time, Glynis had the unshakable impression of piercing, sea-blue-green eyes. The day seemed to brighten, even though the sky was crystal clear already. Glynis's spirits suddenly lifted. Her need to climb to the peak, so intense a moment before, fled from her mind. She turned to head downhill.

As Glynis picked her way downhill along a sketch of a path, she had time to check out the place where the old woman lived. It was a sturdy little bungalow, built in an old-fashioned-looking style. Longer than it was wide, it had a stone chimney on one side and a sundeck fronting the beach. The deck extended from the hill out far enough to need support from heavy pillars. *A cozy enough place if you liked living alone,* Glynis decided.

Behind the house she saw a small shed that butted right up into the hillside itself. The sight of the shed confused her. *That's not right—there should be a cave there.*

Glynis's brow furrowed. *Now why did I expect that?*

Her fascination with the old house was replaced by the wonder of its owner as Glynis reached the deck. Even Todd's careless introduction, "This is Alcina," went by half-unheard as she came face-to-face with the woman in the wheelchair.

Alcina was easily the oldest person Glynis had ever seen in her life. She looked as weathered as her dwelling, but where time and the elements had bleached and reduced the wood to a pale shadow of its former richness, those same forces seemed to have taken this old woman and worn away anything that was soft and unnecessary. What was left were elegantly sculpted forms covered by the barest minimums of flesh. She looked more like fine-grained alabaster than living flesh.

And the way she sat in her wheelchair—back straight, head held proud and high—she might have been a queen upon a throne.

Alcina's hair was a fountain of white cascading down over the faded plaid shawl that covered her shoulders. Her eyes, close up, were indeed a rich sea-blue-green, and their color was echoed in a teardrop-shaped gemstone that hung in a silver setting around her neck. They glittered with a bubbling good humor as Alcina smiled and said, "So you are Glynis. Welcome to my home and may peace be upon you."

Alcina's voice was reedy but surprisingly rich and uncracked. It carried such a sense of self-confidence and command that Glynis automatically replied, "And upon you . . . uh . . ." She flushed. "I guess I mean . . . thanks."

Hearing Todd giggle at her embarrassment broke the spell. Glynis glared at him for a moment before turning back to Alcina. "I'm sorry if Todd was bothering you. He's not really house-broken yet, and I was supposed to be keeping him out of trouble."

Alcina laid her hand on Glynis's, interrupting the girl before Todd could. "Nonsense, child. We were having a lovely discussion about seashells. You are welcome to join us if you wish."

A wave of calm swept over Glynis, softening

what would have been a snappish response. "Shells again? Is he boring *you* about them now?"

Alcina laughed, and the sound was like music. "I fear it might be more the other way around," she said. "I have been filling his head with more than he'd ever want to know about the subject." Her eyes flicked out toward the sea. "The ocean and its life have been a special study of mine for most of my life."

"She even wrote a book about them," Todd interrupted. He patted an oversized volume that lay on the card table next to a tray of assorted shells. "She's lived here forever and knows all about shells."

Alcina laughed again, and the hillside echoed back her amusement. "Not quite forever, youngster, but a very long time by anyone's measure." Her hand caressed the book fondly. "And this is but a small commentary. The seas hold enough to study for many lifetimes, no matter how long they might last."

Todd flipped pages for Glynis. "Look at all this neat stuff, Glyn! Isn't it cool?" Glynis glanced politely at the book. Then she did a double take and looked closer.

The book was as big as one of the oversized atlases in her school library. The paper was unusually thick, creamy in the middle and browned and brittle at the edges. Most of the page space was filled with a large, finely-rendered drawing of a shell, often with different smaller views or variants surrounding the main illustration. The shell's name was printed in antique-looking type toward the bottom of the page over a dense paragraph giving information about its habitat and characteristics.

What struck Glynis the most, however, was the delicate and detailed coloring that had been applied to the printed drawings. That, and the fact that most of the margin spaces had been filled with tiny, precise handwritten notes.

Alcina commented on this before Glynis could. "When this was printed, good tints were not . . . available. I have since painted in the colors as best I could." The woman ran a pale finger over the handwriting. "I also added to the text as reflection and memory served." She looked at Glynis and smiled. "As you might imagine, there is much time to fill when one lives alone."

A strange stubbornness stirred inside Glynis and she gave in to it. "No offense, ma'am, but why spend so much of your life studying shells? It's not like they're any big deal." Todd was ready to throw in his objections, so Glynis hurried on. "I got a lecture on them from Todd last night, but he makes anything he's interested in sound like civilization was built on it." She had meant to sting Todd and was spitefully pleased to see that she'd hit home with that line.

Alcina gave Glynis a sharp look. For a moment, the girl imagined that the old woman's gaze was penetrating her like radar. But then the white head shook a gentle negative and the smile returned to Alcina's lips.

"You may not be pleased to hear it," Alcina said, "but Todd is more right than wrong in this case." She settled back in her chair. "There are many threads that make up the fabric of civilization, and each one had to start somewhere." She waved lightly at Glynis's still damaged watchband. "You yourself appreciate how important weaving was to your ancestors—it gave them the ability to make containers to carry things long distances. Shells provided other threads to other peoples.

"In their simplest service, the animals that lived in shells provided food for people to eat. For many tribes of the original Americans they provided their main sustenance. Whole shells became cups, spoons, dippers, or platters."

Todd chimed in with, "And broken shells were used as knives and scrapers, because the people back then didn't have metal tools."

"Indeed," said Alcina, taking no offense at the

interruption. "And even in places where shells were used mainly for decoration, they were prized for the dyes that could be extracted from them. Murex shells provided a purple color so rich and valuable that only royalty were allowed to wear clothes dyed with it."

"It was called Imperial Purple," Todd added, clearly enjoying having an authority like Alcina backing him up.

"And there were those who saw magical powers in shells," continued Alcina. "Since some shells could be used as trumpets to sound the call to battle, they became symbols of leadership and were held only by chiefs and kings."

"I've seen paintings of ancient Greek sea-gods blowing conch shells," admitted Glynis. "But that's just stories—myths and legends. Reality—that's what's important."

"All myths and legends are ways to explain reality," Alcina explained patiently. "An oyster produces a pearl out of nothing, or so it seemed to the ancients. That was magical to them. And they thought that magical ability was what allowed such soft, boneless creatures to create tough, protective armor. Shells figure prominently in spells for defending the weak and imprisoning evil."

Glynis fidgeted in her seat, so Alcina shifted

her topic by tapping the great book. "But what you should respect more than any of that is how shells represent the unlimited diversity of life." The old woman riffled through pages to illustrate her point. "With only one starting point—a soft animal that needed a protective cover—shells developed in a thousand thousand ways. There are smooth shells, spiny shells, shells that look like fish, and shells that look like rocks. They have adapted to wherever Nature put them and whatever changes were thrust upon them. They have survived and flourished for millions of years."

"Compared to them, we humans are latecomers," Todd enthused.

Glynis pounced. "Is that why you're always late for dinner?"

Todd caught the sarcasm and screwed up his face at her. "No, Commander Snot, I brought my watch today!" He held up his wrist to display it. "That way I won't have to run on Grumpus Standard Time, like you."

Alcina picked up a shell from the tray and pressed it into the boy's upraised hand. "Did you know, Todd, this Spiny Jewel Box comes from just offshore here. And so do those Kitten's Paws." Todd was suddenly fascinated by the delicately colored shell and the sharp projections that pricked his palm.

Glynis realized that the old woman had distracted Todd to nip their bickering in the bud. Since Todd fell for it and began avidly discussing the shells with Alcina, Glynis tuned them out and started looking through the big book. Not really interested in reading the text or the notes, she just glanced at various illustrations, noting how heavy the paper was—much thicker than in any book she'd ever handled before. *I wonder how old this thing is.* She turned to the title page.

It had no illustration on it, only the title in bold letters above a few lines of print: "Shells of the Americas: Being a Description of the Mollusks of the New World." Below that was the printer's imprint and the words, "Richmond, Virginia, 1805."

As Glynis stared at the date, the bright day seemed to dim and an angry heat rose up in her gut. *Wrote it herself, indeed! What kind of dip does she think I am?* She looked across the table at Todd and Alcina. They were smiling and examining the underside of a rose-colored shell. *Look at them, grinning,* Glynis fumed. *They probably think they've played a terrific joke on dumb ol' Glynis!*

She slammed the book down on the card table, rattling the shells and bringing shocked looks to

Todd and Alcina's faces. "I won't let you humiliate me!" she screamed.

"Glynnniss!" Todd squealed.

Alcina said nothing. But a ray of sunlight gleamed off her blue-green pendant and flared to unbearable brightness. Glynis felt a wave of pressure surge into her and strike the smoldering knot inside her chest.

The knot recoiled, yanking Glynis backward away from the table, away from Todd and Alcina, but most of all, away from the awful light of the sea-blue-green gem. Reacting without thought, Glynis turned and threw herself off the sundeck.

CHAPTER
6

Glynis was aware of little as she leaped from the sundeck except that something in the light felt dangerous and needed to be avoided. The same force that yanked her away from the gem also guided the direction of her flight—*uphill.*

The wind in her face as she ran brought tears to Glynis's eyes. Legs pumping like pistons, her lungs burned as she hurled herself up the steep slope. The agony of running filled her body. She was nearly exhausted when she reached the peak.

The oak at the top of Strike's Peak was a monument to stubbornness. Growing out of a sandy patch between the rocks of the summit, it clung obstinately to life despite the forces arrayed against it. Stiff offshore winds had bent its branches backward like hair blowing in the wind. The yearly hurricanes that spun up from the tropic seas to the south had scored its trunk and torn away any limbs unable to bend with the fierce gales. Great vertical splits in the trunk, narrow at their bases and splintered and blackened at their tops, bore mute testament to its battles with the heavens.

The tree's defiance spoke to Glynis. She saw in its scarred form a portrait of how she felt. Those emotions now rose within her and overflowed.

Tears of frustration and misery raged as she threw herself on the tree and hugged its roughness. "I wish I was as strong as you," she sobbed. Salty rivers poured from her eyes and soaked the bark.

Slowly she relaxed. Passion faded into fatigue and sensation returned to her skin. Her internal pain retreated back to a ball of unhappiness and she became aware of an external pain—something sharp was poking into her cheek. She leaned back and looked.

It's that lumpy thing I found the other day! A sober realization set in. *Geez, I could've poked my eye out!*

Glynis looked closer at the lump. The thing inside the bark seemed more exposed today than it had the day before. Something about its shape caught her attention. She started tugging at the fraying fibers, which tore away in ragged strips, then dissolved into a cloud of dusty fragments. Glynis sneezed.

When her eyes cleared, Glynis gawked, astounded by what she saw. Sticking partway out of the solid trunk of the old oak was a perfectly formed seashell. "Well, I'll be!" she breathed. "A whole shell stuck in a tree!" Glynis looked closer. "It's a conch, I think." She remembered seeing a drawing of one like it in Alcina's book.

Better than two-thirds of it remained imbedded in the tree. The exposed section was impressive, though. Almost six inches in diameter where it met the tree, its spire pointed skyward in a graceful left-handed spiral. Small horns and bumps marched along the spire, no two exactly alike in shape or color.

In fact, Glynis was hard pressed to describe the color of the shell. It had a pearly iridescence that shifted in the afternoon light so that it seemed first to be silvery-gold, then rose and amber, and then white and indigo—it changed each time she shifted position.

The color suddenly faded as the sunlight dimmed and a gust of wind blew Glynis's hair in her eyes. Glancing up she saw masses of clouds speeding toward the island from the ocean. Glynis had seen this happen several times during her stay on Seawrack, but somehow this felt different. The way the clouds rushed in made her think of photography, where an hour's movement was compressed into a minute. The clouds were forming long misty fingers clawing out from the east, a sinister inkblot staining the sky.

I'd better get out of here before a storm breaks. She looked at the shell again. *But I'm not gonna leave without that! Todd'll have a cow when he sees it. But it'll be mine, not his!* She grinned, remembering him saying something about conchs never being found this far north. *This'll be something to rub in Mister Know-it-all's face!* She reached out and tugged at the shell.

The oak was not ready to give up its prisoner so easily, however. Glynis realized she'd have to cut it out somehow. "But how?" she muttered, frustrated. The sky was getting darker. There wasn't much time. "How . . . how . . . how—aha!" Glynis grabbed up a chunk of flint with a wickedly sharp edge. She hefted it in her hand once to get its balance, and then started hacking away at the tough oak as if her life depended on it. Strangely, she felt as if it *did.*

"Let! Go! *Tree!*" she grunted, punctuating her commands with heavy chops of the flint.

The tingle of electricity in the air and the distant grumble of thunder only made Glynis more determined to claim her prize before the storm broke. She threw down the flint, grasped the exposed shell with both hands and tugged again with all her might. She cried out in pain as the shell's sharp points cut into her fingers. Bright threads of blood webbed the shell, but that only made her pull harder.

A bright flash lit up the entire sky. Thunder boomed, hard on the flash's heels. The peak shook as if a giant had kicked it. Glynis ignored it all. Her world had shrunk down to the struggle between her and the tree.

Then a sizzling finger of fire lanced down from the sky and the world vanished.

CHAPTER 7

The bungalow was quiet. Neither Michael nor Jaye nor Todd had returned, although it was getting on late afternoon. Glynis sat numbly on her bed, rubbing first-aid ointment into her raw palms. Her hair smelled of ozone and she didn't clearly remember coming home.

But there, sitting on her pillow, was the conch.

It was hard to imagine such a large object being imbedded in wood. *I've heard of tornadoes driving blades of grass or straw into trees,* Glynis thought. *Maybe a hurricane could do it, too.* She looked closely at the shell's mantle. It showed no signs of damage—no cracks, no gouges. Not even the tiniest scratch marred its shimmering surface.

That was another odd thing about it. The room was dark. Glynis had pulled the curtains shut. And yet the shell shimmered all on its own, still shifting colors every time she moved it.

She hefted it gingerly, surprised that such a massive thing could be so light. *I guess it's because it's mostly hollow.* She lifted the shell up and peered inside but couldn't see past where the walls spiraled inward, hiding the inner mysteries. Light shone from beyond that curve. Glynis would have sworn that the center of the shell was *glowing.*

The striping and the curves of the inner surface drew her gaze irresistibly toward the shell's unseeable center. When she caught herself straining to see around impossible corners, she lowered the conch and blinked her eyes to clear them. She felt vaguely cross-eyed and nothing in the room looked right for a minute or two.

After her eyes recovered, Glynis wondered what else she could do to examine the shell. *They say you can hear the sound of the ocean if you hold a shell to your ear,* she remembered with a giggle. *I've never done that before.*

Glynis put the conch to her ear and listened. At first it sounded no different than if she had cupped her hand over her ear—a gentle *sshoooff* kind of hiss. Then she started to hear a rhythm build in the constant sound. *Hah! It's probably just my heartbeat!* she thought skeptically.

But if she concentrated, she could separate out the *lubb-dubb* of her heartbeat from the slower, almost sloshing sound echoing in the shell. *It does sound like waves,* she marveled. A slow grin spread over her face as she listened. *This is cool!*

Glynis sat in rapt fascination, the conch pressed to her ear, entranced by the effect. As she grew familiar with it, she could detect different layers in the sound: a high hissing tone floating over middle *whooshes,* a deeper bass vibration, and random pops and crackles.

Then she recognized that one sound kept repeating—now louder, now softer. It ended in a hiss like so much of the rest of the shell sounds, but it had a more gurgly beginning. She strained to distinguish it from all the other noises in the shell. Slowly it grew clearer.

Glynissss . . . Glynissss . . . Glynissss . . .

The shell was calling her name.

Glynis shrieked and threw it down on the bed, staring at it in horror. For a moment, she had no idea what to do.

Then, on an impulse, she snatched up her pillow and without touching the conch, pushed it into the corner. She buried it under the pillow, then scuttled to the foot of the bed where her duffel bag sat.

The duffel held all the stuff Glynis had packed for the vacation. She wrestled out a clipboard and propped it up against the wall. *I'm going crazy! It's the only way to explain what's doing this!* She unbuckled her watch strap, pinned it under the metal clamp of the clipboard, then rummaged back in the duffel until she found a coil of dried split straw. *This is stupid! I'm* seeing *things, I'm* hearing *things—I have to get a grip. Now!*

Glynis felt calmer as soon as her fingers started unraveling the straw of her watchband. Carefully she teased the broken strands loose and replaced them with fresh straw cut from the coil. The rhythm of plaiting gradually calmed her raw nerves, her fingers repeating their cross-over-cross-under patterns until she could think clearly again.

Try as she might, Glynis couldn't make sense of what was happening to her. The shell's eerie behavior was obviously her imagination working overtime. *I'm so upset about all this family stuff, I'm creating ghosts,* she thought, a little embarrassed.

Dad's got to be noticing this. Eventually he'll see that this is never going to work out. That last thought gave her hope. *And when he realizes that*

I just can't change, he'll have to do something to help me. What her father could possibly do at this point, Glynis didn't know, but she felt comforted anyway. She sank deeper into her plaiting trance. Over-and-under. Under-and-over.

She was just whipping a border around the end of the strap to keep it from unraveling when she heard footsteps on the porch. A moment later Todd came bursting backward into the room, knocking the door open with his back and following through with a spin to drop a double armload onto his bed.

Todd's burden was a pair of thick, flat rectangles topped by Glynis's boot box. Todd picked up the boot box and tossed it over at her. "Heads up!"

Glynis caught the box awkwardly. She was expecting weight but the box was empty and nearly bounced out of her hands. "What's this all about?" she asked. "I thought I was never going to see this again. Lost interest in collecting so soon?"

"No, doofus," Todd laughed as he patted the top rectangle on his bed. "Alcina gave me a *real* display case for my collection, so you get your dumb old box back." He paused, then added in cautious tone, "Uhh . . . she's not mad at you, you know. Not really."

Glynis tried to freeze Todd with a stare. "Why should I care what a dried-up stick of an old lady thinks about me?"

Todd shrugged his shoulders. "Suit yourself, potty-mouth." Suddenly he caught sight of the conch peeping out from under Glynis's pillow. "Whoa! Where'd you find *that?*"

Before Glynis could stop him, Todd leaped across the room and yanked the pillow off the shell. "That's bigger than any conch I've ever *heard* of!"

Glynis jerked to her feet, the knot in her gut churning. She threw herself between Todd and the shell, knocking him backward onto his bed. "Don't you touch that!" she shrilled.

Todd's temper finally flared. "Hey! What is *wrong* with you? You're acting totally weird, even for *you!*" Glaring, he threw the pillow at her, but she neatly dodged it. "And since when did you get hooked on shells? You keep telling me it's the stupidest hobby in the world."

Glynis snatched up the conch and stuffed it deep into her duffel. "It doesn't matter where I got it or why, twerp! It's mine and you keep your grubby paws off it!" She crossed over to Todd and grabbed the front of his shirt tightly, pulling him face to face. "In fact, if you ever say anything about it to anyone—even a hint," she growled,

62

"you won't live long enough to be sorry!" She pushed Todd backward, letting go of the shirt so that he fell heavily on his bed. "Understand?"

Todd looked up at her, truly scared of his stepsister for the first time. "Yeah," he muttered. "Whatever you say." He smoothed his rumpled shirt.

The clump of heavy footsteps on the porch broke the uncomfortable silence. Michael and Jaye were back.

Glynis headed out of the bedroom, glaring back at Todd over her shoulder as she left. "Not a word," she hissed. Todd could only stare, openmouthed.

As Glynis entered the living room, Michael Barrons called from the door, "Give a hand here, will you, Glynnie?" He was struggling through the screen door, pinned by a pair of unbalanced pizza boxes. Behind him, Jaye carried several plastic bags. She rolled her eyes at her husband's predicament.

Glynis rushed over to catch the boxes before they toppled. "What's the occasion, Dad? I thought we were going to make all our meals ourselves." She set the pizzas down on the kitchen table.

"We don't want any cleanup tonight," said Jaye, putting the bags of canned sodas and boxed salads on the counter. "Your dad and I are turning in right after dinner so we can catch the midnight ferry back to the mainland."

"We're leaving?" Glynis exclaimed. Relief flashed through her. "Tonight?"

Her father reached over and rumpled her hair. "Not all of us, silly," he said. "Just Mom and I. You kids get to hold the fort here."

Glynis's spirit plummeted. "B-B-But why—?"

"We signed up for a tour of the state Capitol building," Jaye explained. "You kids didn't want to go and we did, remember? The tour starts too early to make by the morning ferries, so we need to take the last one tonight."

Michael hugged his wife and smiled. "We can take a slow drive through the night and talk for hours like we used to." Jaye gave him a peck on the cheek and turned to open the pizza boxes.

"No fair starting dinner without me!" yelled Todd as he raced in from the bedroom. He threw himself in his chair and started picking at the webs of cheese that hung from a box top.

Glynis was desperate. "But what if there's another sudden storm, like there was today?"

The rest of her family looked at her in puzzlement. "What storm, dear?" asked Jaye. "The weather was perfect today."

Todd choked down a mouthful of pizza in a

hurry to add, "Only storm happened today was when your brain short-circuited, Sis!"

Glynis glared at Todd but bit back her retort by biting her pizza instead.

Michael finished serving Jaye and himself. "If you're worried about storms, hon, we're as prepared as can be." He gestured to the cupboard. "There are hurricane lamps and kerosene in there in case the power goes out. There's also a box of flares so you can signal the Coast Guard if there's trouble." Michael stared directly at Todd. "That's 'real-emergency' trouble, young man, not just 'wouldn't it be cool to light one to see it work' trouble. You catch my drift?"

"Yeffir," Todd said with his mouth full.

Michael turned back to Glynis. "And then there's the modern miracle of radio—you remember, TV without pictures? If you tune it to a local station, I'm sure they'll tell you more than you want to know about what the weather's going to be."

Glynis felt doomed. She ate her pizza in silence as the rest of the family chatted gaily. Todd wolfed down his portion as fast as possible, though Glynis had to give him credit for being less messy than usual. She was shocked when he cleared away his place and actually wiped it clean with a sponge from the sink.

"Now?" Todd asked Michael. Michael, who was barely into his second slice of pizza, looked at the clean area and nodded. "Fair enough," he said. Todd vanished.

Oh no, it's show-and-tell time again, groaned Glynis to herself. Sure enough, Todd came racing back out of the bedroom with an unfamiliar wooden box and something that Glynis did recognize—Alcina's shell book. The boy put the case on the table and leaned the book upright against the back of the chair. He flicked a furtive glance at Glynis.

The box was about four inches deep and was even bigger than the book. It had a pair of glass-fronted doors that could be held open by brass fittings. The interior was lined with faintly yellowed cotton batting, and Todd's collection of a dozen or so shells was held neatly in place by steel T-pins. Under each shell was a label trimmed from index cards with the shell's English and Latin names and the location it was found—all in Todd's tidiest scrawl.

Glynis scowled as Michael and Jaye made approving noises over Todd's accomplishment. Jaye marveled, "Miss Alcina was very kind to lend this to you, Todd." Being a mother, she had to add, "Now, you must remember to write her a proper thank-you note."

Todd nodded his head so vigorously that Glynis thought it would snap off. "She loaned me the book, but she said I could keep the case. She has a whole wall of them in her house. She makes them herself."

"Just like she wrote the book herself?" snapped Glynis. "Better look for a 'Made in Japan' sticker on the bottom."

"You just wouldn't understand about the book," Todd shot back. "You don't understand anything that doesn't go the way *you* think it should!"

"I understand that you're taking advantage of a crazy old crippled lady!"

"Glynnie . . ." Michael rumbled ominously.

"Alcina is not crippled," Todd said. "She can walk perfectly well. She uses the chair so she can save her strength for when she needs it."

Glynis finally lost her temper. "And you're using her to get everything you can from her, just like you're using me and my father!"

Todd's jaw dropped. Jaye turned away from the table and hid her face in a napkin. Michael Barrons's voice cut like a knife. "Glynis Marie Barrons. Wait for me on the porch. We need to have a talk."

Glynis burst into tears and ran out the front door. Behind her she could hear her father making soothing sounds to the others. She stood sobbing at the far end of the porch, never feeling more miserable in her life than at that moment. The knot of tension throbbed deep inside. Why couldn't everything just go away? Why was everything in her life going so *wrong?*

She heard the screen door open and close and then felt a firm hand on her upper arm. "Look at me," her father commanded.

Glynis turned, expecting to see a furious Michael Barrons. He was angry all right, but there was as much confused concern in his face as anger. "What is going on with you, young lady?" he asked, his voice low and clipped. "You were not only completely out of line with your brother . . ."

"*Step*brother!" Glynis interrupted.

"Brother!" Michael snapped. "I adopted him. That makes him your brother." He continued. "Todd aside, you hurt Jaye, and she's never done a thing to hurt you."

The knot in her gut flared and all the emotion bottled up inside Glynis poured forth in a wail. "Yes, she did! She took you away from me! Now I have *nothing!*"

Michael let go of Glynis's arm and took a step back to look at his daughter. "You really think that's true?"

"Well, isn't it?"

Michael's voice softened. "I love Jaye and I love Todd. That doesn't mean I love you any less. We can all be happy together if you give it a chance." He reached out to hug her. "If you feel like you have nothing, it's because you're pushing it all away. No one's rejecting you."

She stiffened in his arms. "I don't want to have to change! I wish *they'd* never shown up!"

Michael had had enough. Gripping her shoulders firmly, he stared Glynis straight in the eye. " 'They' are our *family*. You are going to have to accept that fact and make the best of it." He released her. "Now I want you to stay out here and think about that. I hope that by the time we get back tomorrow, you'll have this all straightened out."

Michael went back into the bungalow, leaving Glynis alone on the porch with the sound of the surf filling the night air. She sank slowly to the floor, huddling into the corner formed by the railing and the house. *Even my own father doesn't understand! I've lost everything good in my life!*

The smoldering knot inside her smiled.

CHAPTER
8

Glynis stayed out on the porch until Michael and Jaye left to catch the midnight ferry. They said nothing to her as they walked past, but Michael looked long and hard at his daughter before disappearing into the darkness.

The bungalow was dark and quiet. Glynis tiptoed through the living room and into the bedroom. Todd lay bundled up in the far corner of his bed, out like a light or pretending to be. Glynis prepared for bed without disturbing him.

She expected that the churning inside her that had kept her out on porch all evening would also keep her from sleeping. But the endless murmur of the surf as it echoed through the house soothed her and she dropped off almost as soon as her head hit the pillow.

Later, it was the sound of the surf that seemed to wake her up, as well. A voice whispered through the soft crashing of the waves. Glynis sat up in bed and strained to hear, but couldn't make out what it was saying.

Slowly, the voice rose in volume. *Glynissss . . . Glynissss . . . Glynissss . . .* Something was calling her name.

Glynis glanced over at Todd's bed, but the boy was deep asleep, snoring. *I don't think even Todd can snore and talk at the same time.* Her eyes raked the rest of the room.

Something at the foot of her bed was glowing, casting flickering shadows on the wall. Glynis scrambled to peer over the footboard.

Stray beams of pale light were streaming out of her duffel bag. Hesitantly, she tugged it open.

Glynissss . . . Glynissss . . . Glynissss . . .

The calling was definitely coming from inside the duffel. Glynis frantically pulled shirts and shorts out of the bag, tossing them on the floor. The light grew brighter.

It was the shell. *Of course,* she thought. As she pulled it out of the bag it shimmered and continued to whisper her name.

Glynissss . . . Glynissss . . . Glynissss . . .

Suddenly Glynis found herself standing on the porch outside the bungalow. She held the glowing conch in both hands as gusts of wind and drizzle plastered her nightgown to her body. *I get it—I'm having another one of those weird dreams!*

And, dreamlike, she realized that the voice calling her no longer came from the shell in her hands. Now it whispered from the churning surf a few hundred yards eastward. Like a magnet, something tugged on the great shell in her hands, pulling it and her toward the water.

The sand was cold on Glynis's feet and goose bumps crawled up her bare legs. The siren call could not be resisted, despite the discomfort, and she staggered slowly forward. The pull on the shell was so strong that she found herself holding it at arm's length, digging her feet deep into the damp sand, trying to slow her momentum.

She was only a few yards from the water when a figure ran past her to place itself between her and the surf. It was Todd.

Again?! Glynis cried in her head. *How can he keep showing up in my dreams?* "Go away!" she shouted at him.

"Don't do it, Glyn!" Todd cried over the rising wind. "Don't let him make you bring it to the water!" He spread his skinny arms to block Glynis's path.

Glynis was confused. She used all her strength

to stop moving so she could sort this out. "What are you doing in my dream, Todd?" she yelled. "Who are you talking about?"

ME, LITTLE SERVANT! a booming voice echoed across the beach. A gigantic shadow rose out of the ocean to tower over the children. It was the shape from Glynis's previous strange dream, only now it was insubstantial and radiated only a faint echo of power. *IGNORE THE OLD WOMAN'S TOOL AND BRING THE SHELL TO THE WATER!*

"I don't understand!" shouted Glynis.

YOU DON'T NEED TO UNDERSTAND. BRING THE CONCH TO THE OCEAN!

"No, Glynnie! Don't set him free! He's really bad!" Todd was crying and shouting at the same time.

SILENCE, BOY!

Todd turned to face the monstrous shadow. "I know all about you! We won't let you free!" he screamed. "I'll tell Glynnie all about you so you don't—"

Todd never got to finish. *No!* thundered the dark giant. A massive hand swept forward, raising a huge wave. It leaped out of the ocean and raced to engulf Todd with the speed of a bullet train.

The sight terrified Glynis. She turned and ran away from the water as fast as she could. The last thing she felt was the beach shaking under her as the enormous wave crashed down over Todd.

CHAPTER 9

Glynis was rudely awakened by a banging noise in the bedroom. Without opening her eyes she yelled, "Todd! Cut that out! I'm trying to sleep!" When the banging continued, she threw the covers aside and leaped out of bed, yelling louder, "I mean it, Todd!"

No answer came. It took her a moment to realize that her stepbrother wasn't in the room. The noise was coming from the window shutter, which was banging back and forth against the bungalow. The wind blew inward, making the curtains billow into the room and the shutter slam closed. Then the wind rushed back out again, plastering the curtains to the screen and knocking the shutter against the outside.

Glynis grumpily slammed the window shut. With the bedroom quieter, she could hear more slamming from other parts of the bungalow. She stomped out of the bedroom yelling, "Is this a barn? How come all the windows are open with this wind?"

No one acknowledged her shout. Then, with a start, Glynis remembered that Michael and Jaye were gone for the day. She was alone in the house except for Todd, who obviously wasn't home.

A quick feeling of unease ran through Glynis. When she had made her wish for everyone to go away and stop bothering her, she hadn't thought far enough ahead to realize that there would be no one to listen to *her* if she were alone. As Glynis listened to the wind slam shutters, she also knew that being alone, nothing would get done if she didn't do it.

Glynis checked the other bedroom quickly and found that window closed. When she went to the kitchen to shut that one, she got her first real look at the weather outside.

"I knew it! I knew it! I knew it!" she hissed.

Gone were the clear blue skies of a summer resort. Gone was the tranquil, if dull, beachscape. Gone was the buttery light of late summer.

The world outside the window looked like it had been designed by an artist with a sullen, vicious palette. The beach and the hills were barely visible beyond streaks of bitter wind. Sand, spray, and debris swirled madly through the air. The clouds above churned violently. The light of the sky shaded from an unpleasant dirty yellow to a brooding violet.

Glynis held her breath as she ran from the kitchen to the living room to look at the ocean. The front door was open, leaving the wind to bully its way in and out of the house through the screen door.

A sudden shift in the wind sucked her out the screen door and onto the porch. Glynis caught on to one of the porch supports to keep from tumbling to the beach beyond. She stared at the ocean.

If the sky was a smeary portrait, the ocean was a battle zone. Every wave wore a whitecap helmet and threw itself headlong onto its neighbor. The front ranks made suicidal rushes up the beach, shattering against the stones but dragging sand back with them to their watery grave.

Glynis was unnerved by the turmoil outside. Her worst fears had come true. *Don't be silly, they said. The weather will be fine, they said! There isn't going to be a storm. Hah!* She bolted from the porch back into the bungalow, slamming the door behind her. *What if Daddy and Jaye are*

76

caught out on the water in this storm? What if they were . . . ? Glynis couldn't bring herself to complete the thought.

"Radio . . . radio . . ." she muttered, dashing around the living room, scanning shelves, yanking open drawers, peeking between knickknacks. Then she saw the portable radio tucked away behind the picnic basket, away over in the kitchen. Leaping forward, Glynis banged her hip into the divider between the living room and kitchen, but she barely noticed the pain. She snatched up the radio and frantically tried to find a local station.

Static hissed out of the speaker until she got a clear signal.

". . . advisory has been declared for the next twenty-four hours. Meteorologists are unable to explain the sudden onset of this storm, but feel confident that traffic between the barrier islands and the coast will be reestablished by tomorrow night at the latest." Glynis's heart sank as the radio announcer continued, "We now return to our regular music programming. Keep tuned for further bulletins."

Glynis ignored the music that began to play brightly from the radio. She paced around the house like a prisoner in a cell. Worries filled her mind. She had thought that being alone would give her a sense of freedom. Instead, all she felt was fearful and exposed. It wasn't till the song ended that she finally noticed the crunch of sand underfoot.

Did Todd track sand through the house? Sure enough, a gritty trail crossed the living room from the door to their shared bedroom. Glynis followed it, distracted from her fears by the familiarity of her anger at Todd. *I should scoop it all up and dump it in his bed. That'll teach the little creep!*

But when Glynis got to the bedroom, she found that the sandy tracks led not to Todd's bed, but her own. She threw back her covers, and stared wordlessly at the still-damp sand lying between the sheets.

Suddenly, she remembered her latest nightmare. "But that was only a dream!" she wailed to the empty house.

Then it hit her—nothing but sand at the foot of her bed? "The shell! Where's the shell?"

At the foot of the bed, all her carefully packed clothes lay in a heap. Glynis tore through the pile in a frenzy. The corner of the duffel showed up, shoved far behind the clothes and under the bed. She jerked it open.

There, gleaming up at her in its own light, was the shimmering shell. Glynis wasn't sure if she should be relieved or terrified, but one thing she did know—"I have to get to the bottom of this!"

Todd would know something about the conch, but where was Todd? It was past noon now and there was no sign in the kitchen that he'd even had breakfast.

He's probably at Alcina's place, Glynis thought. She picked up the duffel, tied it closed as tightly as she could, and headed for the front door.

Glynis was frightened by the storm but she was more frightened to stay home alone. She kept far away from the pounding surf, following a fire trail along the hillside to get as close to Alcina's house as possible before cutting back down toward the beach.

When she climbed up to the sundeck she found the front door to the old house swinging in the wind. She grabbed it and held it still. "Hello?" she called out. No answer. *Maybe she can't hear me.* She stepped inside the house, pulling the door shut behind her.

Glynis stood there, surprised. Alcina's bungalow was quiet. Absolutely silent. It was as if there was no storm outside. She turned to look back out the seaward window to see if the wind had suddenly died down. She frowned at the view. No, the ocean was as choppy as before and the sky was still the same bruised color. But inside the bungalow all was quiet, almost serene.

Did Alcina have the place soundproofed? Glynis wondered. She looked around at the bungalow's furnishings and dismissed the idea out of hand.

Like the sundeck and the pillars that held it up, the wood inside had an oversized, rough-hewn look. The walls and floor were made of wider boards than those used in the bungalow Glynis's family was staying at. The furniture was simple, but had a similar rough construction, though polished to a smooth finish. Something about it struck a familiar chord in Glynis's memory.

It's like the stuff I saw at Old Williamsburg, she realized with a shock. *This place must be old!* Really *old!*

As strange as the interior might be, Glynis had little time to wonder about it. She wanted to find Todd as quickly as possible. She called out again, "Miss Alcina? Yoo-hoo! Anybody home?"

Again, there was no answer.

Her desperation gave Glynis the bravery to poke further into a stranger's home. She saw a hallway leading back into the house and headed for it, thinking it might lead to a back set of rooms. Instead, it led to an open back door, which faced the little shack tucked into the hillside. The shack's door was also open and visible. Just inside it was Alcina's wheelchair. *There she is!* thought Glynis with relief.

Going from the back door to the shack was like dashing through a wind tunnel. Whatever gave the bungalow its calm had no power beyond its doors. Glynis was so buffeted by the wind that she nearly slammed into the door frame of the shed instead of making it through the door itself.

Quiet reigned inside the shed as it did in the house. Glynis's momentum carried her past the empty wheelchair. She was brought up short when she hit the side of the large object that filled the whole back of the shed. She slid to the floor, still leaning against a smooth surface.

When Glynis's head cleared enough to see what she was leaning on, she found it to be a thick slab of glass—one side of a massive glass tank with brass-reinforced edges. There was something floating in the tank, something that was hard to make out clearly because of the rippling effect of the glass and the water inside.

Glynis screamed as the shape in the tank came into focus.

Alcina was lying at the bottom of the water-filled tank, her hair spread like a white anemone around her head. Her eyes were closed and there was a placid smile on the aged face—but she wasn't breathing!

Glynis screamed again and scrabbled frantically to her feet. She ran headlong out of the shack back toward the bungalow. This time, the blustering winds did blow her off-course and she slammed into the door frame at full speed. The world went dark as she tumbled head over heels into the house.

CHAPTER 10

Glynis woke up with a throbbing headache. To ease the pain, she burrowed deeper into the fluffy down pillow. Her right shoulder hurt as well, but there was no give to the wooden floor under it.

Floor?

She sat upright, only to be overwhelmed by a wave of dizziness. Firm hands reached out to steady her. "Be at ease, child," said a calm, soothing voice. "You have taken a nasty fall."

Glynis turned her head to locate the voice. There, kneeling on the floor next to her, was Alcina. Horror returned to the girl's mind. "You're dead! I saw you under water! You drowned! You—"

Alcina laid a warm hand on Glynis's forehead. "Hush now. Fear not," the old woman said. Glynis felt a calm wash over her. She noticed that she had been lying on the floor in the big room of Alcina's bungalow with an embroidered pillow as a headrest.

Alcina rose stiffly from the floor and settled into her wheelchair. "My apologies for the hardness of the floor, young one, but I have no bed to let you rest in," she said. "What brings you here, despite the storm outside?"

Glynis tried to think past the aches in her head and body. "I was looking for Todd. I thought he might be here." Sudden color flushed her face. "The door was open, so I came in." She avoided looking at Alcina. "I don't usually go snooping in people's houses."

"Your brother has not been here today," said Alcina, waving Glynis's embarrassment away. "You are welcome here for your own sake, of course." She peered closely at Glynis. "Something is troubling you. Would you care to tell me about it?"

Despite the calm in the house, or perhaps because of it, waves of conflicting emotions flooded through Glynis. Her lip trembled and tears welled up in her eyes. Whatever had frightened her about Alcina before was absent now. The moment she opened her mouth, the words came tumbling from her lips.

"I didn't mean for something bad to get Todd. It was just that everything in my life was falling apart and he seemed to be part of the reason for it." She covered her face with her hands, crying with full force now. "I'm sorry I made the storm and the giant wave that swallowed him up! I don't want him and Jaye to go away now, really I don't, but how do I stop it?"

"Why do you think you made the storm?" Alcina said. "That is a great blame to take upon yourself."

"I didn't mean to," Glynis sobbed. "It was the shell! I didn't know there was a monster in it! But Todd was so snotty about his collection! I thought it would make him jealous!"

Alcina leaned forward intently. "What shell is this?" she asked carefully.

"The one stuck in the tree on top of Strike's Peak." Glynis pointed limply at her duffel, which lay on the floor nearby. "The one in my bag."

Alcina reeled back into her chair as if struck. She stared wide-eyed at the duffel on the floor. Her mouth worked silently for a moment before choking out, "Show me this thing."

Glynis dragged the duffel closer and dumped its burden on the floor. She heard Alcina hiss in alarm as the great conch rolled out and cast its baleful light into the room. "Poseidon preserve us!" For the first time, the sound of the storm penetrated the bungalow, whining and shrieking, as if trying to break into the room.

Panic gripped Glynis. "What is it?" she demanded, her voice rising shrilly. "What's going *on* here?"

Alcina looked from the shell to Glynis, and the girl felt like she was being X-rayed. A long moment passed. "There is no blame in you," the old woman said finally. "It felt your misery and used it as a lever to free itself." She crumpled into the chair as if exhausted. "My vigil has failed." She closed her eyes and fell silent.

The old house creaked and shifted as the winds buffeted the walls. The windows rattled and the roof moaned. Glynis dried her tears on her sleeve and tried to take stock of what was happening. She looked at the conch on the floor. Somehow, everything that was going on revolved around the shimmering shell. Her nightmares, the storm, Alcina's depression, her burning anger at Todd and Jaye. . . .

Wait a minute, she thought in surprise. *What anger at them?* Sure enough, when she felt inside, she found the smoldering knot that had filled her belly for the past two days was gone. Without the

ball of resentment, the world seemed different—
lighter. She started to feel like her old self. *Why
have I been acting like a whiny baby?* she
wondered.

She looked around with renewed energy and
clearer vision. Beyond the slumped figure of Alcina in her wheelchair, Glynis could see the back
door that faced the shack. Through its window
she could see the shack's open door, and beyond
that, the massive glass tank. The memory of
seeing Alcina floating like the dead in that tank
came rushing back. *I'd forgotten that,* she realized.

*I've been forgetting a lot lately. Something's
been messing with my mind!* Resolve filled her.
I'm gonna get to the bottom of this!

Glynis put her hand on Alcina's. "Miss Alcina?
Ma'am?" Slowly the white head lifted. Alcina's
eyes opened and regained their focus.

Glynis took a deep breath. "In my dream, Todd
said he knew all about the Bad Thing. He said
that 'we' wouldn't let it get free. He meant you,
didn't he?" She looked hard at Alcina. "Tell me
about it. Everything."

Alcina looked at Glynis with tired eyes. "I fear
you are too old and set in your ways to believe,
unlike your brother."

"*Me?* Too old?" The absurdity of the statement
struck Glynis as hysterically funny. Her laughter

rang out through the house, and the very sound of it made the air feel lighter. She stared Alcina directly in the eye. "Try me."

Glynis's challenge energized the old woman. "Out of the mouths of babes . . ." she quoted wryly. "Very well, then." She composed herself in her chair and began her tale.

"In the distant past, great forces, nameless and without form, held sway in the world and struggled with each other as they would. Then peoples arose and began to give shape to these forces, trying to limit those that were destructive and encourage those that were helpful.

"The seas and the lands were ever rivals, each contesting every inch of shore. But the sea-peoples came to realize that neither could exist without the other and that, unchecked, the battling powers could destroy life in both realms."

Glynis's eyes flicked toward the tank. "Sea-peoples?" she asked, hesitantly.

Alcina smiled back at her. "You would call them merfolk, I believe." She patted Glynis's hand. "But have patience. The tale must be told in its own way."

Alcina closed her eyes and picked up the thread of her story again. "The anger of the ocean was a vast and terrible thing in those days. The ancient Egyptians gave it the name Set, the Destroyer.

Their fellows the Greeks called it Typhon." She looked briefly up at Glynis. "You still call some great storms 'typhoons,' in memory of him."

"Him?" interrupted Glynis. "You talk like this was a person or something."

"Not so much a person as a personality, young one. And indeed, he was self-aware and his awareness was anger. He wished to call up the storms of the oceans and the heavens and use them to destroy all life on land. He would be satisfied with nothing less than the rule of a lifeless, churning ocean across the entire world.

"The land peoples could hide from his wrath, for his reach ended at the shore. But the merfolk had no place to hide, being of the sea and the sea being his element. So the king of the merfolk, Triton he was and still is, devised a plan to capture and imprison Typhon and so render the seas safe.

"King Triton possessed a great conch mounted upon a staff that was the symbol of his office and power. He used it to summon all his armies and magic together to do battle with the creature of the storm." Alcina's eyes took on a faraway look and brimmed with moisture. "The battle took years, and many noble folk perished in that struggle. The best and the bravest led the fight and gave their lives willingly for the cause." After a slight pause, she continued.

"King Triton finally caught Typhon by a trick and trapped him in the royal conch. But Typhon was not destroyed, only bound, and the threat of his escape hung heavily on Triton's mind. The ocean was Typhon's element, the source of his power, and many times the storm-thing cast his thoughts into the minds of the weak or unwitting, bidding them to come free him.

"After one such attempt that nearly succeeded, King Triton realized that as long as the sea touched the shell, there remained the danger that one day an attempt might succeed.

"So he called from his people for a volunteer to take the shell and go into exile out upon the dry land, to deprive Typhon of his power and keep him from ever returning to the sea. The king offered to bestow upon that volunteer great magic and power, and the gift of long life, if only they would take this burden upon themselves. He knew that he could not order one of his subjects to do this—it had to be done willingly.

"And a volunteer did come forward, tearfully bidding her family and loved ones farewell. The king himself, with all his court and mages, accompanied her to the shore of a desert isle at the edge of a thinly populated continent. There he strengthened her with magics and they all headed inland in search of a safe prison for the shell.

"They found a cave that led deep into the rock, where the power of the earth was strong and would keep the sea-power away from Typhon. They sealed the cave with wards and spells and built a dwelling before it for the volunteer to live in, a place to keep watch on the evil, that it should never trouble the seas again.

"They gathered at last at the shore for a final farewell. The king kissed and blessed the volunteer before she turned and walked back inland, alone."

Glynis, caught up in the tale, was awestruck by the tragic sacrifice. "And she never saw her home or friends again?"

Alcina's eyes closed. "Oh, they brought her food and comforts for many years. When land folk came across the ocean to settle, her people learned how to build a better dwelling than the original hut." She sighed. "But memories faded over the centuries, and those that were young when Typhon was imprisoned grew old and passed on. The guardian kept her faith, however, though it has been long since she has seen any of her people."

Glynis stared at the ancient woman. It all made

sense now. Her heart ached for Alcina. "How have you survived all these years?"

"Centuries, my child. Many of them. I am old, and weaker than I was, but I am renewed by contact with my native waters."

"The tank—!"

"Indeed. I may not stray so far from my post that I may bathe in the ocean, but I have a system to pump its life-restoring waters up here." Alcina's eyes twinkled. "That is why I could not offer you a bed. Mine would not have suited you."

"And the tank keeps you alive?" asked Glynis.

"As a crumb does compared to a loaf. Should I ever return to the ocean proper, I hope its power in full could restore me to what I once was." Her voice faded to a whisper. "Even if it does not, the choice was mine, and freely made."

Alcina snapped to, fixing Glynis with a blue-green stare. "I have given you the tale of how the shell came to this place. Now you must tell me how it came to be free, and in your bag."

So Glynis told Alcina everything that had happened since her family had come to Seawrack Island. Her honesty forced her to recount every detail, including her petty resentments of Jaye and Todd, even though they embarrassed her now. When Glynis was done, Alcina sat in silence for long minutes.

Then she spoke, and it was as if Glynis was not even in the room. "We thought sealing Typhon under earth would hold him forever. I could feel him in the hill behind me, pushing against me, ever pushing, but I never dreamed that he could use that pushing to make a plant set him free.

"The ages it must have taken to find the right seed, buried under it. To nurture it and make it grow upward, carrying the shell along, until it rose up into the light on the hilltop. I should have realized that the storms were a sign."

Alcina suddenly noticed Glynis again. "Oh, and how he tricked you, my child! Typhon found the coals of your deepest fears and fanned them into a blaze. He drew power from you and used it to manipulate you into setting him free." Alcina looked at the girl with admiration. "But Typhon miscalculated when he chose you, it seems. You never did break and do his bidding."

Glynis was stricken. "But I did! I cut the shell out of the tree and now he's free!"

Alcina grew stern. "Nonsense, child. You only freed the shell. Typhon's power can only be restored if the shell is brought back in contact with the ocean. And this, at every turn, you refused to do, even when he threatened your brother."

Glynis gasped. "Todd! That's right! I haven't seen him since my nightmare!" Fear gripped her heart. "Where is he?"

"HE'S RIGHT HERE," said a rich, gurgling voice from the front door.

CHAPTER
11

On the deck beyond the open front door stood a figure that looked like Todd. Looked like him, that is, if one discounted the unnatural stiffness of his posture, the swirling dark cloud that twisted around him, and the unearthly booming voice that no boy's throat could ever produce.

"Todd!" squeaked Glynis in surprise.

"AREN'T YOU GOING TO INVITE ME IN?" boomed the boy, not moving.

"You know I will not do that, Typhon," Alcina said firmly.

"BUT MY YOUNG SERVANT WISHES TO BE RE-UNITED WITH HER SIBLING."

"Then give him up to her."

"Most certainly, my ancient jailer. Just as soon as the shell touches the sea."

"That I have sworn to prevent at all cost." Alcina sat up straight as a sword. "You are welcome to try your strength against mine, again. You may not enter here."

"The shell is no longer buried under earth. Your people have vanished from the seas. Your powers are gone." Stiffly, Todd's body took a step forward, his joints barely bending. Then another. Without warning, the boy leaped at the doorway.

A blue-green flash of light exploded from the pendant on Alcina's breast, striking the boy's body as it tried to pass the threshold. For a moment the skinny figure hung in green fire before it was thrown back to the deck outside. A howling chord escaped from his throat—the high, frightened shriek of a boy intertwined with the bass roar of fury from the storm-thing enveloping him.

Alcina reeled in her chair for a second, then recovered herself. "My people may be gone, as you say, O King of Liars, but their words still hold."

Glynis thought her heart would break, listening to Todd's screams. She snatched the shell from the duffel and stood with it held high over her head. "Let Todd go," she shrilled, "or I'll smash your rotten old shell!"

The Todd-thing's only answer was an earthquake-sized laugh that rumbled through the bungalow like a train.

Glynis threw the conch down as hard as she could. It hit the floor with a loud *TUNNGG,* bounced once, then came to rest, still whole.

Glynis looked at it in wonder. Its surface didn't even show a mar, much less a crack or chip. The ancient wooden floor, however, showed a deep, pale gash in one plank. *No!* her mind shrieked. *This isn't fair!* A familiar ugly knot formed in the pit of her stomach. It almost made her sick.

Alcina was staring at the cloud swirling around Todd. She raised her pendant to her face, as if sighting a weapon. Glynis heard Alcina's voice dimly through a rising red fog. "His power is confined to the shell, child. As long as he dwells in it, it cannot be destroyed. What you see outside is only a projection, a tentacle cast out to try to twist the world to his will." A blue-green beam leaped from the pendant toward Todd, boring its way through the dark cloud surrounding him. "Give up the boy, Typhon!" she commanded.

The Todd-thing had stopped its laughter. It stood up on the deck and moved closer to the door, staring directly at Glynis. An invisible smile in the cloud surrounding the boy grew broader and hissed, "YESSSSSSS!"

Glynis's anger grew, both at the thing outside and at herself. *Okay,* she admitted to herself, *I was stupid to expect the shell to break on wood.* She looked at the fieldstone fireplace. *Let's see how well it holds up when I smash it against* stone! She reached down to pick up the conch.

Absorbed in her contest with the storm-thing, Alcina realized too late what Glynis was about to do. Glynis heard the old woman shout, "No, child! Do not—!"

Then the whole world turned black as her fingers touched the shell.

CHAPTER
12

Glynis floated in a whirling vortex shot through with violet streaks. The only sound was a slow repetitious, *SHHH-THUMK! SHHH-THUMK!*

Jagged flashes of light seemed to shoot through her but she felt nothing. She had to concentrate just to force a coherent thought through the numbness. *Where . . . am . . . I . . . ?*

She noticed the repeating noise. *Is that my heartbeat?* She decided to go looking. She felt herself drifting like a tiny mote in the great ocean that was her own body. Ribbons of color swirled by as she moved. None of the colors seemed bright and pure, but were murky and contaminated by flecks of black and red. She followed the

99

ribbons as they twisted around themselves and pulsed toward a large object that loomed ahead.

Now that she was closer to it, Glynis could feel enormous waves of sound and vibration from the object. Forcing her brain to work, she finally interpreted the *lubb-dubb, lubb-dubb* ahead of her. *That's my heart!*

Once she defined it, it came into clear focus. But it didn't look the way illustrations showed it in science class. Instead, Glynis saw her heart as a massive, living pump that never ceased. She could feel it as it moved blood throughout her body. On another level, as if animated on an overlay covering her view of the heart, Glynis could see the ribbons of color collect around it and then go out again, following different paths than the blood.

Glynis tried to understand what those ribbons were. Then, like moving from static to a clear station on a radio, the knowledge came to her. *Those are my emotions!* she thought in awe.

The awe soon gave way to dismay, however, as she realized that none of the ribbons were bright and cheerful. Nearly everything she saw was either anger or unhappiness. The realization so upset her that Glynis let herself be swept away from her heart by the pulsing of her blood rather than face all that pain and anger.

Which is how she felt herself descending to her feet, where she found the source of the *SHHH-THUMK, SHHH-THUMK* sound. *That must be what walking sounds like from inside,* she thought. *But where am I walking?*

As if in answer, Glynis suddenly felt her perceptions shift. She could feel her arms and legs again. The real world reappeared, seen through her own eyes. The sound she'd heard was her feet as they slowly, stiffly walked across the sandy beach toward the ocean.

Glynis watched her own hands stretched out, holding the conch before her. The shell pulled at her like a tow rope, dragging her body behind it as if she were a marionette. She lurched forward. Her legs, heavy and clumsy, swung out just in time to keep her from falling. The shell was forcing her, foot by foot, toward the water.

The storm raged around her, bright lightning flashing, and deafening peals of thunder rolling past. Impossibly huge breakers smashed onto the beach ahead of her, dissolving into foaming chaos before sliding back under the next furious wave. Her senses felt muffled, though, as if she were peering out through a dark cloud that enveloped her.

As she had in her vision of her inner world, Glynis saw colors overlaying everything she saw.

Is this what they mean by "second sight"? she wondered. The shell in her hands looked like a tornado of blacks and purples, twisting and writhing within the confines of the conch. And there was a thick, twisty rope of grainy red-black that ran from her heart to the shell.

The horror of it slowly dawned on Glynis. *That Typhon-thing is making me take the shell to the ocean!* Fear shot through her, a jagged feeling that added a ribbon of purple to the rope between her heart and the shell. *But at least if it's got me, then it'll probably let Todd go.*

Glynis was surprised to be cheered by that thought, and even more surprised to see it become a brief flash of gold filling her heart. *So that's what* hope *looks like,* she marveled.

But the ribbons of darkness and anger quickly smothered the gold and left Glynis feeling more lost than ever. The feeling of doom swept from her heart into the shell, and Glynis could have sworn that the shell then *pulled* a stream of seawater out of a wave toward itself.

The salty water drenched Glynis and she heard a great soundless snapping that seemed to rock the world

"FREE! FREE! FREE!" the voice of Typhon boomed.

Glynis felt power rush out of the conch into

the ocean. Offshore, a mass of water started to swell, rising up and taking on shape as it grew taller. Forty, fifty, a hundred feet it rose up from the waves, taking on human shape to loom over the shore. Glynis tried to scream, but terror choked her. *It's the sea-thing from my dreams!*

The man-shaped mountain of water that was Typhon lifted his mighty arms, one at a time, and the waves lifted in response. He clenched a fist and a bolt of lightning arced down from the sky to blast a rock on the beach. "THE POWERS OF THE STORM PRIMEVAL ARE MINE AGAIN! THE CLEANSING OF THE WORLD SHALL BEGIN!"

A spear of blue-green light lanced across the beach and struck the towering figure. Typhon reeled backward with a furious roar.

Alcina stood on the beach, her white hair whipping in the wind, shining pendant raised high in her hand. "No! I shall not allow it!" she cried.

Typhon bellowed in anger and reformed himself. He shook his watery fists and a hail of lightning fell down upon Alcina. The green beam from her pendant became an emerald bubble, deflecting the thunderbolts to the beach around her, where they blasted craters in the sand.

As Typhon drew in his power to hurl it at Alcina, Glynis felt his control slip away. She still had that curious double vision that let her see extra colors in the world, but her thoughts and body were her own again.

"You are old and weak, water-woman!" Typhon thundered. "Your long stay on land has dried up your power! you are no match for me now!"

"Is that so?" Alcina's blue-green bubble became a shield and lance. The lance stabbed at Typhon again and again, blasting huge gouts of water from his body, while the shield continued to deflect the storm-thing's lightnings. Alcina walked toward the water, each step won against Typhon's power. "The ocean that restored you, Typhon, will restore me also! You will be bound again!"

"Then you shall never reach the sea!" bellowed Typhon.

He lifted his seaweedy arms high and drew the waters back toward himself. Glynis gasped as the surf retreated, leaving a quarter-mile, then a half-mile, of suddenly exposed seafloor between himself and Alcina.

Despair washed over Glynis, her double vision coloring it a sickly yellow. But as fast as it formed, the yellow was sucked into the rope between her heart and the shell. In response, Typhon swelled larger.

"Take this for good measure!" he boomed. He raised one foot to stamp the seafloor and an earthquake rolled forward, rocking Glynis and throwing the frail Alcina to her knees. Alcina's green shield flickered.

He's feeding off of me! Glynis realized. *He's using my emotions to fight Alcina!* Typhon's distraction allowed her to think clearly for the first time in days. She realized that the storm-thing had preyed upon her resentment and unhappiness since that first day up on Strike's Peak. Now she could see how he had stoked her anger and then sucked it from her heart to add it to his own strength. She felt a calmness wash over her. She hefted the conch. *I'll show him the puppet can pull the strings* back!

Without pausing to think or to feel, Glynis hurled the shell down on a rock. As it shattered into a thousand glittering fragments, Typhon roared as if mortally wounded. His sea-form lost shape and started to slump back into the ocean. The colored rope between the shell and Glynis's heart snapped, throwing her backward onto the sand.

"I did it!" she cried in triumph.

But then Typhon conjured up a ball of purple storm-fury and cast it at the shore. It splashed down over the shards of the conch, coating them with crackling energy. Glynis gasped. Like a film running backward, the fragments rushed toward each other and reassembled. In moments, the shell was whole again and its power shimmered brighter than before. Out in the ocean, Typhon rose again, smaller than before, but more furious than ever.

Glynis had failed to destroy the shell, but at least her actions bought Alcina time to renew her attack. The merwoman hurled her magic at the storm-thing, holding him back—barely.

Old weed-face doesn't have me to pull strength from any more, Glynis thought grimly. *But there's got to be something I can do! I've got to make him pay for what he did to Todd!*

An unexpected vision of Todd leapt into Glynis's mind. She imagined him smiling at her and yelling, "Kick his soggy butt, Glynnie!"

"You bet I will, Todd!" With that positive thought, the golden glow of hope filled her heart. The last grainy strand of despair snapped.

As if feeling Glynis's freedom, Alcina shouted, "Typhon is tied to the shell, child! Bind him to it, destroy the shell and he will be banished forever!" The merwoman threw a green bolt that sent Typhon reeling. "Hurry!"

Tied to the shell? How? Glynis aimed her double vision at the conch lying several feet away. With effort, she focused until the shell filled her field of vision and tried to see what made the shell glow. Magnified, the shimmering resolved into innumerable energy-threads, much like the emotion-threads Glynis had seen in her own heart. The threads ran over the outer and inner surfaces of the shell and then, pouring out of the hole, formed a cord that stretched out toward Typhon in the ocean. She could feel the flux of power as it moved back and forth between the storm-thing and his former prison. *So that's how he does it!*

While tracing out the threads, Glynis felt herself automatically sorting them by color and density, grouping them into strands held in imaginary fingers. She could actually *feel* them and was amazed when she found they responded to her imaginary movements. *Boy, will Typhon be surprised when he finds that two can play his string game!*

Then her concentration snapped as Todd thumped down on the sand next to her. Under one arm he carried a bundle of red waxy sticks. Before Glynis could yell at him for interrupting her, he gasped, "Flares! Burning it's the only way to destroy it!"

Glynis immediately squelched her anger and tried to regain her focus on Typhon's energy threads. She was dimly aware of Todd lighting one flare after another and forcing the flaming ends under the conch, but she couldn't risk dividing her attention again. Her job had to be done *now.*

Glynis concentrated and the glowing threads snapped back into her awareness, still sorted as before. *If I can plait these strands into a loop, Typhon will be stuck without a place to go when the shell burns!* She started laying one set of strands over another, tugging them into tight knots. Her imaginary fingers moved as quick as thought.

There were strands that carried power out to Typhon and different strands that carried power back. Set by set, Glynis teased them free and spliced their ends together to form loops. With each new closed circuit, she could feel the great storm-thing lose some power.

Typhon felt it, too. His bellow of rage nearly deafened the two children on the beach. Swinging a great arm, he called down a flood of rain on Glynis and Todd. The force of the water pummeled Glynis but did not stop her. She heard Todd shout over the downpour, "Don't worry, Sis—flares are magnesium! Water can't douse 'em!"

Glynis barely heard him as she continued her task. The loose ends were splicing together faster and faster now. The bottom of the conch was glowing red-hot, despite the torrent of rain. She could feel the figure of Typhon out in the ocean start to shrink.

That same sense warned her that he was clenching his fist to bring bolts of lightning down on her and Todd. *Uh-oh! We've had it now!* she thought, but still continued to braid.

The boom of thunder and the shaking of the beach told Glynis that the lightning had struck. But she was still alive. A quick glance upward showed her a shining blue-green dome keeping the deadly bolts away. *Good old Alcina!*

That gave her an idea. Reaching out with her mind, Glynis snagged some of the pendant's energy and started weaving it into a cocoon around the conch. She remembered the odd pattern of the rotted fiber that had surrounded the conch when it was trapped in the tree, and she imitated that pattern.

The magical pattern of the ancient weave did its work. Glynis could feel Typhon being pulled back into the shell as the green wrapping neared completion. The heat from Todd's flares was reducing the conch to white powder. No matter how Typhon struggled, Glynis's braiding and the green wrapping kept him contained and bound as the flares destroyed his shell. His bellowing grew fainter and fainter until it was nothing more than a desperate, whispery shriek.

With a sudden *CRACK!* the shimmering shell crumbled to dust. The green cocoon fell inward upon itself and vanished with a soundless pop.

And for the first time in her life, Glynis Barrons fainted.

CHAPTER
13

Wake up, Glynnie! Wake up!"

Glynis opened her eyes to find her head pillowed on Todd's lap. Tears fell from the boy's eyes onto her face as he kept sobbing her name. Glynis looked up at him. "Chill out, little . . ." Her face broke into a smile. ". . . brother."

She sat up slowly and looked around. The ocean was calm and blue and the last of the clouds were rapidly dissipating. A few feet in front of her lay a small pile of white powder. Todd walked over to it and kicked it with the toe of his sneaker. "Want some calcium carbonate?" He grinned. "Makes great fertilizer."

Glynis chuckled weakly, then stopped short

when she saw the body lying limply on the beach. "Alcina!"

The old woman lay on her side, her face in the sand. She looked drained and as pale as a shell herself. Together Glynis and Todd ran to her and gently turned her over. A weak croak issued from her throat. "Sea . . . water . . ."

Todd ran like the wind to the surf, stripping off his T-shirt as he went. He soaked it in the water and ran back up the beach. His face grew red as he wrung the shirt out with all his might over Alcina's face and body.

Both he and Glynis held their breath as they waited for some reaction.

Slowly, color returned to Alcina's cheeks and her eyelids fluttered. "Carry me to the sea," she said.

Glynis grabbed Alcina under the arms and Todd took her feet. The old woman seemed to weigh less than nothing. Moving crabwise, they carried her easily down to the surf line and lowered her into the foaming water.

A small wave broke over Alcina, covering her face completely. Glynis fought back the urge to snatch the woman out from underwater. Then the wave receded and both children gasped.

Bone-white hair turned a rich seaweed green. Wrinkles vanished from the ancient face, Alcina

112

still looked like there wasn't an excess inch of skin on her, but she glowed with renewed golden vitality. Her eyes fluttered open and she smiled.

It was like the sun had suddenly come out. Glynis felt her heart would burst with happiness. Alcina slowly stood up, her feet still in the sea. Her fathomless sea-green eyes looked from Glynis to Todd and back again.

"You have done well, children," she said. "Better than well. You have helped banish from the world a terrible danger." Tears filled the mermaid's eyes. "And you have made it possible for me to go home."

Glynis knew her heart was breaking now. Todd was openly crying. Glynis had to ask, even though she already knew the answer. "Do you *have* to go?"

Alcina turned to stare at the endless movement of the ocean. "I have not seen my people in more centuries than I can count," she said. "I may be the last of my kind." She lowered her head. "I hope that I am not."

Alcina turned to look at Glynis and Todd again. "But I will never forget what you have done for my world and your own." She lifted the pendant from around her neck and held it in front of Glynis. "Look into the stone, child."

Glynis looked at the sea-green stone in its silver

setting. In its depths she could see threads of deeper greens and blues moving in the slow rhythms of the tides. "The ocean changes constantly," Alcina said to her, "but never loses anything of itself as it does."

She turned to Todd. "You already have my book. What was a loan is now a gift," she said, hugging him.

Alcina stepped back and smiled at Glynis and Todd. "Gifts await you both back at your home," she said. "Perhaps they will bring us together again someday."

Still beaming at them, Alcina walked backward from the two children deeper into the water. Before they could react, she ducked from sight under the cool waves.

She broke the surface once last time, far out to sea, restored to her full youth and original form. She slapped the water once with the broad tail that her legs had become and then dove deep beneath the waves.

Glynis and Todd stood hand in hand staring out at the ocean until the sun dropped below Strike's Peak behind them.

Wordlessly, they trudged back home.

CHAPTER
14

Cheery yellow light spilled out of the bungalow windows as Glynis and Todd stepped on the porch. Glynis's combat boots clumped in time with the scrunch of Todd's sandy sneakers. Glynis no longer had double vision to see the energies around things, but she could feel the potential for happiness in the snug house. It almost made her giddy.

There was a message light blinking on the answering machine in the living room. Todd headed into the bedroom as Glynis pushed the Play button. Jaye's voice came from the machine.

"Hi, kids! Just calling to check in. We'll be back this evening, right on schedule. Heard that you might have had a run-in with some bad weather today. Hope it turned out okay. Love and kisses!"

"Love and kisses . . . Mom," Glynis whispered. She reached out to press the Rewind button.

"Glynnie!" came a high-pitched shriek from the bedroom.

Glynis was in the bedroom in a flash. Todd stood in front of his bed, his mouth hanging open in shock. "What's the matter?" Glynis asked breathlessly.

Alcina's big book on shells lay open on his bed. Todd pointed wordlessly at the piece of parchment spread over the pages. Glynis leaned forward to read the neat, old-fashioned script:

To Whom It May Concern,

My work here being done, I hereby bequeath my house on Seawrack Island to the Barrons family for their use in perpetuity. I especially bequeath my collection of shells and all their accompanying notes to Todd Barrons, in the hope that they will encourage him in further study.

It was dated and signed, "Alcina de Mer," in a flourishing hand.

Glynis was still speechless in wonder when Todd tugged on her sleeve and pointed to her pillow. Glynis turned to look.

There, gleaming softly in silver and blue-green, was Alcina's pendant.

Epilogue: The Midnight Society

Well, we could probably wish that the story would end with Glynis and Todd being best buddies and never fighting again. But we all know how likely that wish is to come true.

And what about Alcina's wish to find her people? If you wish for it, I might be able to tell you a story about that. Another time, of course.

I declare this meeting of the Midnight Society closed. Because it's getting late, you see, and much as we'd wish that our time could last longer, it's time to go home.

Alone.

In the dark.

Wish you luck. . . .

ABOUT THE AUTHORS

Stolen from Gypsies as a child, DAVID CODY WEISS was raised in suburban comfort until his teens. Then his true heritage claimed him and he broke loose of the middle-class straitjacket, going forth and having many jobs (no two alike!). When he acquired a wife (and partner), he decided that becoming a writer was better than working for a living. His goal is to become independently wealthy, and he thanks you for buying this book.

Delivered one Christmas morning by reindeer instead of a stork, BOBBI JG WEISS has spent most of her life avoiding reality, and to this day she still keeps up a personal correspondence with Rudolph. Clinging to the belief that cartoons are real, that cats speak English, and that coffee bestows superpowers, she is fit for no profession other than that of writer. With her husband she has penned novels, comic books, animation, trading cards, CD-ROMs, and dumb little comic strips for orange juice cartons. One day she hopes to *become* a cartoon.

THE HARDY BOYS® SERIES By Franklin W. Dixon